SHOULDERS OF GIANTS

SHOULDERS OF
GIANTS

SHOULDERS OF GIANTS

THE DEMON GATEKEEPER: BOOK TWO

RUSSELL BROWN

www.blkdogpublishing.com

For June & Gordon, Mum and Dad.

I stand on your shoulders every day,

and for Geordie, we all stand on your shoulders.

The Demon Gatekeeper Book One:
War of the Wolves

Lewis saw the wolf because he couldn't sleep.

Lewis didn't believe in magic. Not until he was chased by a man who could change into a wolf. Not until he discovered he could change into one too. Not until he was told that he and his friend Charlie were the only ones that stood between a demon and the end of the world as they knew it. Now he believes. Now he has no choice.

Now he'll need to learn what it means to be a magical creature in a secret world at war. Now he'll need to discover how to control his new found magical powers, and learn how to fight monsters, hell bent on trying to destroy everything he loves. The only problem is, it's sometimes hard to know who the monsters really are.

ON THE ISSUE OF BLOOD POWER

There are many theories as to why blood power acts the way that it does, and is generally weaker in smaller magical creatures and increases in power and potency the larger the creature is. Some believe that it is weaker in lesser magical beings due to the type of body it inhabits. Others believe that it becomes distilled over time as smaller beings are not able to contain the power. That it will fade away into nothing after a certain number of generations, eventually leaving the likes of flutterbys and imps as normal beings with no magical properties at all. The theory goes that the greater the body mass, the more able the creature is to retain blood power and pass it on through the generations. If we follow this theory through to its logical conclusion, it would mean that giants and trolls should be the most powerful creatures on earth. But they are not. As we know, werewolves and lycans are by far the most powerful creatures and royal lycans the most powerful of all. This theory doesn't take into account The Source or the fact that demons feed off lycans and werewolves, but nothing else. In conclusion, these theories around size and body mass are incorrect.

And yet, we do know that blood power has a gradient of potency that does generally follow size. To start with, all magical creatures have blood power. It's what makes them magical. Smaller creatures such as imps, and sprites have what appears to be the smallest amounts. How do we know this? By the sense of potency they give off. This potency increases as the creatures become larger, such as drakes, trolls, unicorns etc. But it also varies according to type. Goblins are more potent than water nymphs but are clearly smaller. So, once again, our size and body mass theory is blown out of the water. A messy business if you're a water nymph. So, what *does* potency depend on? We only have theories. What we do know is that the strongest blood power stands with just two beings. The blood royals themselves. Thanks to their victory over the demon Blaine, we now know that demons need to feed off lycans or werewolves in order to sustain themselves on the earth. We also know that Blaine had been doing this for centuries before he was sent back to hell.

We also know that The Source, that incredible tree, living underground and protected by satyrs, is where all blood power originates. But we cannot feed off it or take power from it by force. Not even demons can feed off it. We can only receive its gifts. But not everyone has received the gift of blood power. Humans, the most populous creatures of all, have no blood power and don't even believe that magic exists.

In conclusion, blood power enables magical creatures to be magical. It originates from The Source. There is a potency gradient, albeit inconsistent, and blood royalty are the most powerful creatures on earth. Demons can only feed off werewolves and lycans and need to feed in order to remain on earth. Which leaves us with one final question – now they have been banished, will they ever try and return?

Section taken from the publication On the Issue of Blood Power *by Derek Smyth, Blkdog Publishing, 2025.*

DRAMATIS PERSONAE

The lycan lashed out with his claws and missed the werewolf's face by inches. After regaining her footing the werewolf roared in response and dived towards her enemy, ducking under another swipe of his claws and smashing into his chest with force. The momentum catapulted them both over the edge of the cliff, but the werewolf managed to grab hold of an outcrop of rock halfway down and control the rest of her decent. When she reached the bottom, she landed lightly on her hind legs, and began to search for her opponent. It didn't take long to find him, lying face down on the floor, one arm jutting out at an unnatural angle. He'd changed back into a human and his breathing was short and laboured. The werewolf also changed back into a human and crouched down beside him. He was lying on his stomach with a band of thick black hair covering his face. She brushed it aside to reveal a pale face etched in pain.

'Why do you still attack us, even though The Dark Man has been sent back to hell?' she asked.

'You're an abomination,' he said through gritted teeth.

'I'm not an abomination, my name is Amelia and I like fast cars and slow boys.'

'You're a werewolf who followed a demon.'

'So, you're a lycan who followed a demon.'

'We didn't know what Blaine was.'

'Oh, come on, it wasn't hard to tell. He'd lived for thousands of years and had red eyes.'

'It doesn't matter, he's been sent back to hell too.'

'Yes, by the blood royals, quite a duo you've got there.'

Amelia reached out and turned the lycan onto his back. He let out a grunt of pain but said nothing.

'That's better, I can see the whole of your face now, you're a mess by the way, the fall was a bad one.'

The lycan remained quiet.

'I could help you, but seeing as I'm an abomination I won't bother. Tell me what are they like?'

'Who?'

'The blood royals.'

'Powerful,' the lycan said, wincing as he turned his head.

'I heard that. Only just turned seventeen and already powerful enough to send demons back to hell.'

Like most of her fellow werewolves, Amelia had heard how Lewis and Charlie, the blood royals, had sent her master, The Dark Man, back to hell by reaching inside him with their minds and crushing his heart. It had been a blow to hear what had happened. Like her companions she had run away from the site of the great battle between lycans and werewolves when she found out. The fact that giants had come to fight on the side of the lycans, had encouraged her to run faster.

In the six weeks since that battle, she'd also learnt that Blaine had been sent back to hell by the pair, and that Bob, the leader of the lycan crew, and the blood royals' second in command, had taken over the shop Blaine once owned.

It had been a terrifying time for Amelia. She had hidden in the sewers below Glasgow, too scared to walk the streets in case she was captured by lycans. Then she'd heard that Mr Mono, The Dark Man's assistant, was alive and back in Glasgow Zoo, The Dark Man's abandoned hide out. She'd rushed back, hoping to find others and to her delight, many of her werewolf companions had found their way there too. Mono had promised them that he would help The Dark Man return and told them to go out and take the fight to the enemy. That was what she'd done, and now she'd found herself sitting on the ground talking to a dying lycan.

'What's your name?'

'Curly.'

'Hello Curly, I wish we could meet under better circumstances, but you're the enemy and I have to kill you, Mono's orders.'

Curly just stared at her and said nothing, once again.

'Still, I don't see why we can't have a chat before I send you on. I hear you have humans working for you now, is that right?' Amelia asked.

Curly continued to stare.

'Come on, there's nothing wrong with being polite, even when you're dying.'

He closed his eyes and let out a low moan, before opening them again. 'Yeah, we have a human working with us.'

'Who is he?'

'Derek, he's the leader of this group that explores old places in Glasgow.'

'I think I might have seen them one night, a small bunch of nerds in yellow anoraks, why are they working with you?'

'I don't know, I just do as I'm told.'

'What about Calder, is he still working with you?' Amelia asked through gritted teeth. Calder Rouge was the great betrayer. He was supposed to identify the blood royal Lewis so that The Dark Man's werewolves could go and capture him, but he'd warned him, and his lycan friends, of the danger instead. Even worse he'd told the lycans where The Dark Man's hide out was. That had been a dangerous mistake that meant Mono had to kill Calder Rouge's family. Amelia didn't know how she felt about that, but she knew that Calder was a traitor and deserved a traitor's death.

'I haven't seen him,' Curly responded weakly, 'I've been busy visiting a bunch of lycan families to tell them that their loved ones have died, and searching for you lot.'

'Don't worry, we'll find him.' Amelia said, half to herself.

'Why do you follow him?' Curly asked, before a coughing fit overcame him.

Amelia knew the lycan didn't have long and she needed to get as much intel from him as she could, but she couldn't resist rising to the bait.

'Why did you follow Blaine?' she hissed. 'He was a demon and kept my master in hell for as long as he could. At least The Dark Man never hid his true nature, we always knew what he was. Blaine pretended to be on your side when he was only in it for himself. He was feeding off your blood power and you didn't even notice. We gave our power willingly and he rewarded us for it.'

Curly made no response, he simply stared at his enemy.

Amelia shook her head in frustration, the lycans never understood what it was like to sit at The Dark Man's feet and feel the power that surrounded him. The werewolves took comfort in that power and fed off his confidence and surety, it gave them a purpose.

'So, you're all living at the shop, now Blaine's gone?'

'Yes, where are you hiding?' Curly asked weakly.

'Mono likes his privacy; sorry we don't want a horde of lycan's descending on us.'

'You're afraid of us, aren't you? You're afraid of the blood royals' power.'

'We fear no one, we just don't want you lot sniffing around,' Amelia said, with a confidence she didn't feel. She was sure Mono was as afraid of the blood royals as she was, and that this was the reason why they kept their hide out a secret. Unlike the lycans who did nothing but party in that shop of theirs.

'So, what are you lot planning Curly? Are you going to try and find our hide out and attack us?'

Curly didn't respond. His dead eyes simply looked up into space.

'Damn it!' Amelia cursed, she had so many more things

she wanted to ask him, but she wouldn't get the chance now. With a sigh, she stood up and walked away, leaving the body for the crows.

BACK, LET'S GO BACK

T he car's headlights brushed off the wet surface as it sped forward, illuminating arrows of rain that quickly disappeared under the bonnet. Water drummed a steady beat on the roof, echoing inside the silent interior and increasing the tension.

A man, a woman and a sleeping boy occupied the inside. The two adults stared intently out into the pouring rain, each trying to see through it into an uncertain future. The man gripped the steering wheel tightly, his eyes darting from the windscreen to the speedometer and back again at regular intervals. The woman sat as still as a statue, in the passenger's seat, a grim line marking the place where her mouth should be. They had been sitting that way for some time now, while the car kept a steady speed down the empty road, neither wanting to break the tension, neither wishing to wake the boy.

'You had to tell him, didn't you,' the woman whispered, finally breaking the spell.

'I had no choice; he was going to find out anyway.'

'You don't know that. He could have just been fishing. He probably knew nothing.'

8

'He knew,' the man replied with certainty.

'Well, he does now,' the woman huffed, turning her head and staring out of the window.

'This could be a good thing,' the man replied, gripping the steering wheel tighter.

'How on earth is running away in the middle of the night a good thing?' the woman asked, turning back around to star at him.

'You said you wanted to get away from it all. To give him a normal life. Now we can.'

'Living hand to mouth on the run isn't a normal life.'

'We don't have to live that way. We can settle down somewhere no one knows us. We can start again, as a proper family,' The man said, trying to placate her.

'We need money and new identities. New national insurance numbers and passports. Do you have all that in your back pocket?' the woman asked.

'No, but I know where we can get them.'

'Maybe you should have thought of that before you opened your mouth and we had to run. Anything illegal we do now will surely tip them off to where we are,' the woman said, shaking her head in disbelief at his answer.

'I did what I thought was best,' the man said, through gritted teeth.

'No you did what suits you, as always,' the woman replied, pursing her lips.

'Do you think this suits me?' the man replied with anger in his voice.

'Don't play the innocent with me, that's the one thing you've never been. Everything you do is for selfish reasons.'

'I'm doing this to save you and the child.'

'You're doing this to protect your legacy. Don't pretend it's for our benefit.'

'So why did you come, then?' the man asked, shrugging his shoulders.

'Because you gave me no choice, you idiot. You revealed the one thing you needed to keep secret, you told him about our son.'

'He knew, I've already told you!'

'Stop shouting dad,' the boy said sleepily, from the back seat.

'Keep it down,' the woman hissed at the man.

They sat in silence for another few miles, the tension slowly rising once again.

'What's that behind us?' the man asked, after another mile of tense quiet.

The woman stared into the side mirror intently. 'Obviously, it's a car.'

'Yes, but how long has it been there?'

'We're on the motorway, it's probably been there for some time.'

'It's closing in on us fast.'

'Cars tend to do that on the motorway.'

'No, I mean it's getting closer really quickly,' the man said with rising panic.

The woman turned around and stared out of the back window. 'Put your foot down,' she said in an urgent whisper.

'I'm already doing 80.'

'Then do 90! I think it's them.'

'How can you be sure?'

'Just a feeling, go faster,' the woman said, staring intently out of the back window.

The man put his foot down and the car sped forward. It didn't work. The chasing car continued to close the gap.

'Can't this go any faster!' the woman hissed.

'We'll take off if we go any faster.'

The car continued to gain on them, the headlights growing in their rear view mirror. The man tried to speed up, but their car wasn't as powerful as the one chasing them. After a few more miles, the cars made contact, both veering off the road at speed, smashing through the barriers and rocketing into a field beyond. The man tried desperately to control the car, but it was no use. The vehicle skidded into the field and rolled over several times before coming to a stop, steam hissing from the radiator and one wheel slowly grinding to a stop in the dirt.

Luckily the boy had fallen back to sleep, so his limp body fell into the well between the seats and he escaped unharmed. The man lay unconscious across the steering wheel, blood pouring from a cut on his forehead. The woman lay with her head back, her hands resting in her lap.

'Mum,' the boy moaned gently. 'Mum, what happened?' No reply came from the woman in front.

'Dad, I hurt my arm, what happened?' Still no reply from the front. After a few more seconds of silence the boy climbed out of the well and fell onto the back seat. He looked up to see both his parents lying unconscious in the front and let out a whimper of fear. For a few moments he sat there quietly, not sure what to do. Then he heard a low growl coming from outside and looked up to see two red eyes staring at him. He slid to the other side of the car and pushed opened the broken door. Spilling out into the field, he gathered himself up and began running. Without thinking he ran into the night, the image of the red eyes spurring him on.

It was hands that eventually stopped him, pulling him back into the arms of a strong embrace. The boy screamed and tried to break free, but the arms were strong and held him tight.

'Shush, you're safe,' the voice belonging to the arms said. 'Hey, stop struggling, you're safe. I'm not going to hurt you.'

'Let me go,' the boy wailed.

'OK, I will, but stop struggling first. You're safe now.' The arms released the boy and he fell to the ground. 'Are you OK?'

'Let me go,' the boy said again.

'I'm here to help you and your mum. She's OK but she needs help.'

'My mum's, OK?'

'She's alive, but we need to get her to a hospital.'

'My dad, too; he's hurt.'

'We'll see.'

'There's someone out there,' the boy said in a trembling voice.

11

'It's OK, they're gone now. They can't hurt you. Come on, let's get your mum and you to a hospital.'

'My dad too.'

'Yeah, like I said, we'll need to see about that, Lewis.'

The boy stared at the stranger with wide eyes, somehow, he knew his name.

OPEN GRAVE

Charlie stood on the edge of the grave and watched her tears drop into the abyss. She felt empty. A hollow vessel. A dry container that used to hold love and affection, but now held nothing, not even air. She didn't notice the people surrounding her, or the hand that was resting on her shoulder. All she could see was the grave in front of her, now filled with her gran's coffin. It felt strange to view that simple wooden box, sitting snugly inside its dark brown tomb, and think that her gran was inside. Her loving, supportive, affectionate gran. The woman who prised her out of bed in the morning, scolded her when she forgot to do her homework and warned her against wearing ripped jeans and loud makeup to school. The woman who had held the wolves at the door, literally, her whole life.

Lewis squeezed her shoulder and whispered something in her ear, but she paid him no attention. Her body was fixed to the spot, her mind was elsewhere. She didn't notice as the service ended and the minister shook her hand and told her he was sorry for her loss. She barley registered the hugs and soft words from her distant relatives and didn't realise that fine rain was falling until it began to soak through her clothes.

'Charlie, we have to go,' Lewis said quietly, for the millionth time. She didn't respond. He hadn't expected her to. He took her hand gently and slowly pulled her from the graveside. She resisted at first, but he insisted, and she followed him without comment. They were nearly at the car when she stopped.

'Charlie, we have to go. They'll be waiting for you at the wake.'

'I need to go for a walk. I just need to clear my head. I'll catch up with you, promise.'

'That's not a good idea. You're already being watched by those social worker types. If they think you're acting suspicious, they'll put you in a home or something. Best to get this over with and keep everyone happy.'

'Happy?' Charlie mused. What was that? She vaguely remembered something called happiness a long time ago. But that had been destroyed by a monster with red eyes. All she knew now was loss and hurt. 'Yeah I know, and I promise I won't be long. I just need a bit of time by myself.'

Lewis sighed and nodded. 'OK, five minutes, we'll wait here for you.'

Charlie smiled thinly and turned away from him. She knew he was only trying to help, but there was no helping this. The only family she'd known had been taken from her by a demon who'd pretended to be her friend, and she was alone, totally alone.

Charlie was small for someone who was supposed to be a mighty blood royal. Standing just over five feet tall, her frame was clothed in a white blouse, black skirt and black jacket, but the rebel in her couldn't resist wearing a pair of red boots, just to get the oldies talking. Jet black hair surrounded a pale face containing ice blue eyes and red lips. Charlie nearly always wore a smirk or a grimace on her face but today she had the haunted look of someone who'd lost everything. She walked across the empty graveyard and before she knew it, she was in the trees on the opposite side of the street, the lush greens enveloping her like a balm on an open wound. She sighed and let them take her. After the brief euphoria of beating the demons, the last six weeks had been a blur of crying, wailing and hugging. She welcomed the calm of the woods. The gentle swaying of the branches and the whispering of the wind amongst the leaves soothed her troubled soul. She felt a small sense of peace for the first time since she found out that the demon Blaine had killed her gran, in order to stop her revealing that he was a demon who fed on the blood power of the lycans. He'd probably killed her parents too, for the same reason. She also felt some comfort in the fact that she'd helped to send him back to hell. She knew this feeling of peace couldn't last, however. She would have to go out and be Charlie. Even worse, she would have to be the blood princess they all expected. All she wanted to do was run away. To become a nobody once again, pleasing no one but herself, defending no one but herself, responsible for no one but herself. Then she thought of Lewis and remembered she could never escape. She could never leave him alone to face an uncertain future. Beating The Dark Man and Blaine had given them a respite from the war, but it hadn't ended it. The creatures had been sent back to hell, where they belonged, but they would return, that was certain. The question was how to beat them once and for all when they did.

She didn't hear the noise at first, it was just part of the rustling background in the trees. Then the growling became louder, until it turned into a snarl, that turned into a roar. Charlie swivelled around to meet the challenge and by the time the werewolf reached her she was no longer a vulnerable teenager, she was the blood princess. It never had a chance. Its head was detached from its body by the time it finished its charge.

She watched the head roll to a stop at her feet without emotion, the face looking up at her. It changed quickly into that of a girl, her dead eyes staring off into the distance.

The second werewolf dived at her from behind. With supernatural speed, Charlie spun around and smashed it across the chest as it came in close. The creature was sent sideways, crashing into a tree before crumpling to the ground.

It changed as it lay there, becoming a weak and shivering man, holding his arms across his chest. Charlie changed and crouched down in front of the dying man.

'Why did you attack me?' she asked quietly.

He looked at her through pain filled eyes and laughed weakly. 'You're my master's enemy; we have sworn revenge on you and the prince.'

'The battle's over, he's been sent back to hell. You know you can't beat us, so why try? It'll only end in your death.'

'He commands and we obey. We are legion, my princess, and we will have our revenge. Look to yourself. He is coming.'

'You poor misguided fool,' Charlie said, shaking her head.

'We are one,' he replied quietly, sighing as life left his body.

'What the hell does that mean?' she demanded, shaking the lifeless corpse. 'Come on you idiot, tell me, what does that mean!?'

'Charlie,' Lewis said quietly, entering the woods, crouching down and putting a hand on her shoulder.

She looked at him with tears in her eyes. 'It's never going to stop, is it?'

'Not until we find a way to kill the demons.'

'It's such a waste. There's no reason to any of it. They can't beat us, I don't know why they even try.'

'Because they believe in him. As crazy as it sounds.'

'Why believe in a demon, I'll never get that.'

'For the same reasons we believed in Blaine. We trusted him, we thought he had all the answers, we thought he could help us and care for us.'

'I never trusted him.'

'No, you didn't; that makes you by far the smartest person in the room.'

'How on earth do you kill a demon that's already in hell?'

'I have no idea, but I know a man who does. Come on, we need to get to that wake thing before people start asking questions.'

'Yeah, let's go and eat cake and drink tea. That'll put everything right,' she replied cynically, wiping tears from her eyes. 'What about them?'

'No problem, Bob can deal with them.'

'OK, let's go,' Charlie said, taking a final glance at the dead man at her feet. 'It's enough to put you off your steak pie, that is.'

RUMBLES IN THE DEEP

'You will tell my wife I love her, won't you?' the man asked, his eyes wide.

'I'll make sure to tell her,' his companion replied, taking him by the arm and guiding him through the door into the abandoned station. The smell hit them first, a mixture of rotting leaves and vinegar that made both of them gag. The red eyes hit them next, six perfect pairs running along each wall. The man stopped in the doorway, a thread of fear running down his spine.

'Come on, it won't take long. They're not here for you, I promise.'

'No one said anything about werewolves.'

'It's part of the ceremony, but don't think about that, think about your family. Think about all the things that money will give them. A moment of pain will give them a lifetime of luxuries.'

'You promise?'

'You've seen the contract. It's been signed. There's no going back on it unless you go back on your word. You don't want that do you? You don't want your little girl to suffer?'

'No, I don't want that.'

'Remember the money will buy her the best of health care. She can go private and get all the treatment she needs right away. No more waiting on the NHS and all that. It's in the contract.'

The man nodded. Swallowing hard he made his way into the room.

A space in the centre had been cleared of rubbish and replaced with a wooden table, that had candles burning at each of the four corners. Standing at its far end was a silent figure that looked like a robot. His skin had a silver tint, and his mouth had a fixed look that gave the impression it had been painted on. Only his eyes gave any indication of life. But their colour told of a soul as black as night.

The man hesitated in front of this strange sight, unsure of how to react.

'You need to lie down on the table, Tom,' his companion whispered in his ear.

'Er, yeah, right,' Tom replied, before carefully making his way onto the table.

His companion nodded once to the silver man, then made his way towards the exit.

The silence enveloped them all. Only the hissing of the candles as they burned, and the occasional grunt from around the room, broke it. After a few more moments, the silver man stepped forward and looked down at Tom's horizontal form.

'Do you come here willingly?' he asked in a flat tone.

Tom nodded once, licking his dry lips and trying not to look up into the nostrils of the strange man who now stood over him.

The man stared at him for a moment, his cold eyes boring into Tom's upturned face, then he nodded and stepped back out of sight.

'Sa comes sabbia willingly haeng,' Tom heard the man say behind him. He instinctively wanted to turn around and look at the man making the strange sounds, but he knew if he did, they might not honour their side of the bargain. A bargain made with a pin prick of Tom's blood. He needed them to honour the bargain he had struck, for his daughter's sake.

'Qota yiz sacrifice zes haeng. Maph mnaez zhaeaeg willingly. Qota ednardhy mnaez iq aes Azazel. Yaeza ynaeuks yiz koqa oth qota esaeun rightful k'oya.'

The candles suddenly flared into life, exposing the werewolves surrounding the table. They all roared in unison and fell to the ground, barking and whining in agony.

Tom clenched his fists and tried not to think about the monsters surrounding him. He concentrated on the face of his wife instead, her soft loving eyes and warm smile.

The man appeared over him once again, this time holding a golden sword that seemed to glow in the candlelight.

'You are a servant of Azazel,' he said. 'You serve him willingly. Now is the time to give of your blood, now is the time to serve.'

It all happened quickly after that. The silver man raised the sword up over his head and plunged it down and into Tom's heart in one smooth motion. A cold pain erupted across his chest, and all the air left his body. It took a millisecond for him to realise what had happened. He opened his mouth to scream but it didn't respond. A strange feeling of detachment flowed over him, and he realised with a start that he couldn't feel any pain.

'You can get up now,' the silver man said from behind him.

Tom sat up and swung himself off the table. He had been told that he wouldn't feel much pain but hadn't really believed them. He was relieved to find out they'd been telling the truth. A smile spread across his face. He'd done it. He'd met his side of the bargain. His daughter would be safe, and his family would be as rich as Midas. He couldn't wait to go and tell them the good news.

'You have fulfilled the contract,' the silver man said. 'You are now part of the void. Look upon yourself and weep.'

Confused, Tom followed the line of the silver man's pointing finger. At first, he found it hard to comprehend what he was pointing at, then reality struck him and he collapsed to his knees. His body was still laid out on the table, the golden sword piercing him through the chest. From his prone position he could see that it had gone straight through him, and the table, pinning him to it. Blood was dripping from the tip and pooling underneath.

'I'm dead!' he managed to gasp.

'You are now in the void,' the silver man replied. 'Look upon your work, small man, look upon that which you have released.'

The ground began to rumble. A deep sound that shook the rubbish across the floor and made the table rattle on its legs. He looked across the dancing legions of dirt and rubbish as they jumped in unison and watched the werewolves on the opposite side of the table all fall to the ground in a writhing mass of burning flesh. A thick, oily cloud filled the room, its surface punctured by the flashing orange of flames, as they consumed their victims on both sides of the table.

Tom gagged, despite the fact that he was dead and shouldn't really be able to smell anything. He scampered across the floor and curled up in a corner of the room, looking on in horror as the werewolves continued to burn. After a few more minutes of chaos, the screaming died down and the smoke started to clear. Tom could make out a lump on the table where his body used to be. It started to tremble, then bulge. A hand shot up, quickly followed by an arm. A leg appeared, then another one. It shuddered towards the edge of the table then flopped off, hitting the floor with a plop. It's legs and arms continued to grow, then a back appeared, and finally a head.

'Master?' the strange silver man said. 'Master, I am here.'

'Mono,' the head said in a strange whisper. 'Where are we?'

'We are at the final portal my master. We have brought you back to your rightful home.'

'Why did you take so long?'

'We had to find the sword, and a willing body. We went as fast as we could.'

'Not fast enough. I have suffered Mono, you cannot begin to understand the depths of my suffering.'

'It is over now, you are home.'

The lump slowly stood up and stretched out its arms, bones cracking as it did. It rolled its neck and let out a sigh of contentment.

'Why are we here and not in the city?'

'Their hold is weak here, my master.'

'So far away. Have we come so far?'

'It was necessary to avoid detection.'

'Yes. We'll meet them when we are ready. When they least expect us.'

'Blaine is gone master.'

'His suffering will make mine look like a splinter. It's no more than he deserves. We must take control while we can, there's no telling when he will make his way back. He always was the most cunning of us all. My other brothers are in need too, we must be careful.'

'We are ready master, you need only command.'

'Where is my army?'

Mono paused before replying. 'Much reduced, my master. We suffered a heavy defeat in the woods.'

'Then we must gather more.'

'As you wish.'

'Where is the surrogate?'

'Hiding in the corner.'

'Get rid of him, I don't want anything left behind.'

The silver man looked towards Tom, his face set firm, his eyes empty. 'It is time to fulfil your commitment,' he said, striding towards Tom with purpose.

STEAK PIE AND MUSHY PEAS

Calder stared at the dark brown gravy, pooling on his plate, and sighed. He hated steak pie. He hated the soft mushy vegetables that always accompanied it, and he hated the bits of gristle and fat that stuck in his teeth. But it was a staple for a Scottish funeral wake, and he wasn't about to rock the boat. He sighed once more and picked up his fork. He started to shovel food into his mouth, not caring that he was dripping gravy onto his raincoat. Calder always wore his favourite caramel coloured raincoat whatever the weather, and the same grey suit with a nearly white shirt and a tartan tie handing loose. He'd never been too bothered about his appearance, but he'd let himself go since his family had been killed. He was unshaven and his salt and pepper coloured hair was a mess. His eyes were bloodshot from too many sleepless nights and too much whisky, but since the funerals, he needed it to numb his senses. He'd been to too many lately. You expect to attend more as you got older, but you didn't expect to go through what he had over the past few weeks. The last one had nearly sent him over the edge.

No father should be made to stand at the side of their child's grave. He'd wanted to jump in and join his son. The fate of the world might be on a knife's edge, but it could take care of itself. There was nothing left in it that he cared about anyway. The darkness would have been a blessed relief. He'd felt his feet slowly tip over the edge, and would have followed them, if it hadn't been for Bob grabbing him at the last moment.

A hole had opened up inside Calder the moment he'd been told that his wife and children were dead. Killed by Mr Mono, the silver-coloured monster who served The Dark Man. A yawning chasm that no amount of wailing or crying would ever fill. He'd felt broken from that moment on, moving from day to day in a dream-like state. He ate when his body told him he had to, and he slept when he couldn't keep his eyes open, only to be awoken sometime later, screaming and reaching out for the children who were no longer there. Food had no taste, and the sky had no colour. The sound of people's voices became muted, as if he was submerged under water. All he could smell was the copper scent of death, and all he could think of was the sounds he imagined his family had made, as they had pleaded for their lives.

He'd thought that sending Blaine back down to hell would have been revenge enough. But it left him feeling just as empty as before. So, he'd started to look for Mono, so he could make him suffer the way his family had suffered. But he couldn't find the monster, no matter how hard he searched. He spent his time wandering in dark places, hoping that he would show himself, but he never did.

'The peas are nice,' Bob said.

'What?'

'The peas, they're nice, you should try them. Put some vinegar on them, it makes them taste even better. They'll give you terrible flatulence but no one's perfect.'

'I'm not really that hungry,' Calder said.

'You're missing a treat. If you don't want yours, I'll take it?'

'Be my guest.'

'Nice,' Bob purred as he reached across the table and took Calder's plate.

'How long do you think this will go on for?'

'Why?'

'I need to be somewhere else.'

'Where do you need to be?'

'Just somewhere.'

'He won't be there, wherever you're going.'

'You don't know that.'

'Yes, I do. No one's seen him since the battle. He's powerless without his master, and he knows we're looking for him.'

'Someone told me he'd be at the station.'

'Funny that, someone told me he'd be at the zoo.'

'Really?' Calder shifted closer to Bob.

'Yeah, and the graveyard, and the slaughterhouse. They're just rumours, I told you, we'll find him when he makes a mistake. It's only a matter of time. You just stay where you are. I think it's apple pie for afters.'

Calder stared at him intensely before replying. 'No, I need to do this. For my family and for myself.'

'Fair enough,' Bob sighed, turning around to tuck into his second plate of steak pie.

'What, that's it? You're not going to try to persuade me to stay?'

'Nope. You've clearly made your mind up, there'd be no point.'

'I see. OK I'll see you later then.'

'Hang on Calder,' Lewis said, appearing from behind him and siting down.

'Be quick, I've somewhere I need to be.'

'Don't we all. The last time you went to speak to The Gatherer, didn't he tell you things about Blaine's sword, when you gave it to him?'

'Yes, but this isn't the time or the place, I'll speak to you back at the shop later on.'

'No this is exactly the time and place. We're at this funeral because of what Blaine did, and we need to make sure nothing like that happens again,' Lewis said.

'What about the sword?' Calder replied with a sigh.

'It's the only thing that can bring him back from hell, right?'

'Yes.'

'But can it kill him?'

'Yes, I think it's the only thing that can.'

'I mean properly. Not send him back to the pit, but end him?'

'Yes, it will kill him. The Gatherer said it was the one thing on this earth that would end his life on all planes of existence.' Calder replied.

'What about the rest? Can it kill them too?' Lewis asked.

'I don't think so. The sword was Blaine's, it contains his true essence, that's what makes it such a dangerous weapon.'

'So what kills the others then?' Lewis mused. 'If he has a weakness, perhaps the others do too.'

'I don't know. I never thought to ask,' Calder said with a shrug.

'Well, perhaps you should have? After all, we know they're all trying to get out of hell. Maybe the only way they can do that is if they have something like swords too. And if they do, perhaps they can be used to kill them,' Lewis suggested.

'Maybe. That would make sense, they're all demons after all. But if that's the case you'd have to find these artefacts, and I wouldn't know where to start looking.' Calder said.

'I do,' Bob interrupted, 'we can start the search by making another trip to the station, but don't worry Calder, we'll come with you this time.'

'Super,' Calder said with a sigh.'

Midgy shifted in his seat. He hated funerals. His gran always made him wear a shirt and tie when he attended one. He didn't look good in them. He was tall and thin, with a messy head of brown hair and eyes that seemed to stand out of his head. His nickname captured his features well, he looked like an insect with his eyes standing out on stalks. To make matters worse, being tall and thin meant clothes just seemed to hang on him. One of the Knight Shift (the self-appointed corridor heroes tackling demons and werewolves at Midgy's school), remarked that he looked like a bag of crap tied up with string. They weren't far wrong. The thought of the Knight Shift made him feel sick. Three of them had been killed the night the werewolves attacked his school. The rest had been rescued when Midgy turned into a lycan and killed the marauding band of monsters, but he'd not been quick enough to save some of his friends. He felt their loss deeply and vowed to find out where the monsters had come from, and why they'd attacked his school. That was one of the reasons why he sat there in a suit and tie. That and the fact that Charlie was his cousin, and her gran had been his gran too, although he'd not been as close to her as Charlie had been. He was far closer to his other gran, his dad's mum.

He looked across at her, sitting on the opposite table, and sighed. She looked like she was just about holding it together. The pain of the past few weeks was written in bold letters across her face. Charlie had been close to her gran after her parents had died. It was the same for Midgy. He'd lost his parents when he was young. He could only remember his mum's soft loving eyes, and his dad's strong embrace. Since then, it had been him and his gran against the world. Her loving support had been all consuming. The thought of losing her made him shiver.

He felt nothing but sadness as he looked across at Charlie. He could never imagine how he'd cope if he had to go through this himself. He wasn't even sure he'd be able to attend the funeral if his gran passed away. He was in awe at how well Charlie was holding it all together. He didn't want to disturb her, but he needed to speak to her urgently. Swallowing hard he made his way over. She didn't realise he was there at first, her eyes were glazed over, her fingers playing absently with crumbs on the table. He coughed lightly and sat down next to her.

'Hi Midgy,' she said with a weak smile.

'Hi. I'm sorry about your gran, she was a lovely person.'

'Thanks,' she replied, pain etched across her face, 'she was your gran too.'

'Yeah I know, but I didn't really know her all that well. My other gran and her didn't get on and she was too busy looking after you. Look, I know this is probably not the right time, but I need to talk to you about something.'

'Sure, what is it?'

'Well, it's hard to explain, and it's probably going to sound mental, but...'

'You were attacked by a group of werewolves while you were at school?'

'Yeah. How did you know?'

'I heard about it from Bob.'

'Who?'

'The funny looking guy over there,' Charlie said, pointing absently across the room at a man wearing a green jacket and red trousers.

As far as Midgy could tell, everyone across the room looked funny, but he didn't say that out loud. 'Anyway, I've been speaking to my gran and she says you might be able to help.'

'How can I help?'

'Well, it isn't just the attack that's the problem. I mean it is a problem and we want to find out who they are and sort them out, but that's not all of it.'

'They're dead,' Charlie said blankly.

'What do you mean?' Midgy asked, a shiver running down his spine.

'The ones that attacked the school. They're dead.'

'How do you know that?'

Charlie leaned over the table, a menacing smile spreading across her face. 'Because I killed them.'

Midgy stared at her, his expression blank.

'I know what you're thinking. How did I manage to kill those monsters? Well, it's easy when you're a monster too.'

'You're a lycan aren't you?'

'How do you know about lycans?'

'Because I am one.'

Charlie looked confused for a second, then understanding spread across her face.

'Your gran explained it all to you after you changed for the first time?'

Midgy simply nodded in reply.

'Welcome to the madness. What else did she tell you?

'That you and Lewis are some kind of royalty and you've won a great victory.'

'Not so great, but I think it helped.'

'I need to know what it is I'm getting into Charlie.'

'So, you're not that bothered that you can change into a great big dog?'

'No I'm terrified. I'm trying to understand what's happening to me, but I need to know everything else. How much danger am I in, and what can I do about it?'

'Did your gran tell you anything else?' Charlie asked.

'Not much. She said I was special. That I was a lycan and there are loads of us. Like I said she told me about you and Lewis and that's it.'

'It's all about magic and power, blood power to be more accurate. We have it and demons feed off it. The demons are our real enemies. The werewolves are kind of like their soldiers.'

'How many of them are there?'

'I've no idea how many werewolves there are. All we know is that there are nine demons, and most have been sent back to hell.'

'Nine!' Midgy said, his eyes bulging even more than usual.

'Yep. We're not sure how to kill them, but we can send them back. The only problem is, they keep escaping and getting into our world. That's what we need to stop.'

'We were just playing at all this in the Knight Shift. This is way more dangerous than I imagined. I just wanted to find those werewolves and finish them.'

'What's the Knight Shift?'

'Just a bunch of us from school who got together to

protect the place and the pupils. You know how there's been strange things going on for years?'

Charlie nodded. 'It's much bigger than a few werewolves attacking the school. Look I think we can help you Midgy. Help with controlling your power. I think you can help us too.'

'How?'

'You said you wanted to hunt werewolves; I can help with that.'

A wide smile spread across Midgy's face. 'That would be cool.'

IMAGINARY FRIENDS

Derek always wore a suit and tie, even at home, and always had his hair combed back, to reveal a shiny forehead and a mass of worry lines. He never wore rings or a watch and thought tattoos were the mark of the devil. He had a plain looking face, but his mouth was forever turned up into a leer. To Derek most people were beneath him and the leer told them so.

Sat alone in his living room he whistled a bright tune as he carefully polished the railway sign. It was his favourite. A rare example of a sign from a bygone age, and as far as he was concerned it was priceless. He'd found it, abandoned, in his favourite lost place, Buchanan Street Railway Station, a forgotten station now submerged beneath shops and pavements in the heart of the city. He rubbed lovingly along the smooth, cream coloured surface, feeling the raised letters as he moved along. It had just been a rusty sign when he'd saved it. Now after months of care, it had been brought back to its former glory. The shiny black letters evoking images of simpler times, when folk knew their neighbours, and looked out for one another. When butter was cheap, salmon was expensive and you could ride the bus for 2p. A time when there were no monsters or magic.

He shivered at the thought of the monster rampaging through the sewers. One minute it was a kid, the next it was a hulking wolf with bright blue eyes and sharp teeth. He'd been certain the thing was going to eat him and spit out the gristle.

'You'd have known how to take care of that thing, wouldn't you, my love?' he said to the empty room.

For a second, he half expected a reply, but Cindy was dead, consumed by a cloud of neon coloured monsters who'd dragged her down a dark lift shaft. Derek still wasn't sure how he felt about his girlfriend's death. On the one hand, he missed her laugh and her quirky smile, but on the other, it was far better that she was dead and he was alive. He shuddered to think about the members of Abandoned Glasgow, crawling through his stuff and dividing it amongst them if he'd died. They had no idea what the true value of his treasure was. What was a pile of junk to most people was a catalogue of Glasgow's lost past to Derek. A priceless hoard of memorabilia that captured a bygone age. He was particularly proud of his railway signs. He'd been told by one of the younger members of the group that they were going for thousands on the internet, but Derek didn't believe him. Besides, he would never part with his precious signs. Each one was a memento of the place he'd rescued it from. He remembered Cindy pointing out the one he now held in his hands. He sighed once again at the thought of her. It was such a loss. She'd been such a silly girl. He rubbed the smooth surface of the sign as his mind wandered once again to that awful night. He could still feel the pain of a thousand creatures attacking him all at once, their heavy bodies covering him in a blanket of angry light, their legs crawling over his skin, trying to pry open his mouth and his eyelids. He shuddered at the thought and grasped the sign hard.

'They can't hurt me, they're all dead,' he said to himself. 'Cindy killed them when she took them down the lift shaft.'

'I might not have killed them all, my love,' the voice whispered across the living room.

Derek yelped and dropped the sign. Before he knew it,

he was cowering in a corner, his hands held out in front of him. 'Who's there?' he demanded.

'Have you missed me, my love?' the voice whispered in reply.

For a moment, Derek wasn't able to speak, his brain taking a while to compute what he was hearing.

'Did you miss my kisses, Derek? I bet you did. I'm so much better at it now. I can make all your fears go away with just one kiss. Would you like me to show you, my love?'

Derek could only respond with a squeak. He wasn't in complete control of his body at that moment.

'Don't be like that, my love, I know you've missed me, I've missed you too, even though you've been a very naughty boy. You didn't try very hard to save me, did you? And you left me down that deep dark hole; what a naughty boy.'

'I didn't abandon you,' Derek managed to squeak. 'You were already dead.'

'That sounds like abandonment to me,' the voice replied with a chuckle.

'Why are you doing this?' Derek moaned.

'Because I can, you selfish little man. I know what you were thinking – better her than me. Better for her to die, so I can live. That's terrible, Derek. What a coward you are. You haven't even gone back to retrieve my body, or told the police what happened.'

'I am not a coward,' Derek replied, finally getting back some of his courage. 'I went to that crazy man in the shop, to find out what all this was about. He sorted out your body, or so he said.'

'But you never went back for me, did you? You were too afraid to look into the abyss.'

'What do you want?'

'For you to make amends my love. Prove to me that you're not really the pathetic loser I think you are.'

'Cindy!'

'Finally, you say my name. Took you long enough.'

'How can I make amends?'

'You can give me a kiss,' the voice whispered.

'How can I kiss you when I can't even see you?'

'I'm over here, silly, right next to your favourite toys.'

Derek turned his head to look over at a range of signs attached to the back wall. At first he couldn't make anything out amongst the riot of reds, greens and blues. Then he saw a set of black eyes staring at him intently.

'Cindy?' he said.

'Ah, you found me, well done. Now, come over here and give me a kiss.'

Derek tried desperately to resist the urge to move towards the voice. Something screamed at him from the back of his brain, telling him that his life was in danger, and he needed to get away. But her voice was seductive, and he needed to see the face at the end of it. He needed to give Cindy a kiss and tell her he was sorry for being such a selfish coward. His limbs began to move on their own, making him take a staggering step towards the eyes.

'That's it. Come closer, my love. I'll give you a kiss so deep, you'll forget who you are.'

Derek's head began to wobble as his brain tried to resist the voice. His limbs however seemed no longer to be connected to him. They moved forward of their own accord, the screaming inside his head getting louder as he took another step forward. He could make out red lips and a button nose now, all framed by an angular face, crowned with those jet black eyes.

'Just a few more step and we'll be together forever, my love' Cindy whispered.

'But — you're dead,' was all Derek could say, as he strained to make his limbs stop.

'You say the nastiest things,' Cindy replied with a chuckle. 'Come over here and make it up to me.'

It was at that moment that Derek realised two things; the voice wasn't Cindy's and he was going to die. His body took another step forward as the revelations raced through his brain. He tried everything he could to stop his limbs from moving, but they felt like they we held in a vice. He had no control over them, no matter how much he tried.

'Don't resist, my love, you always loved my kisses; when you could be bothered that is,' the pretend Cindy said with a chuckle.

'Stop it,' Derek whispered through gritted teeth. 'Let me go,'

'Why, when we are having so much fun?'

The knock on the door was loud and insistent and Derek instantly felt free from Cindy's iron grip after it rang out. He jumped back from the pretend Cindy and fell to the floor.

'No, come here, my love, we're not finished.'

'I have to see who it is,' was all Derek could think of in reply. He dived for the living room door and barged his way out, just as another loud knock rattled the front door.

'Derek, are you there?'

'Oh, thank God,' Derek rasped as he opened the door. 'Jamie! Please come in.'

Jamie come through the door, quickly followed by another taller man, with dark black hair and eyes full of suspicion.

'Marco! Glad to see you,' Derek said, the relief at being free from Cindy's control flooding through him.

'Er, hi, Derek,' Marco replied, surprised at the warm welcome.

'Come through, quickly, you two, something strange has happened.'

'Again?' Jamie asked.

'Just come through.'

Emboldened by the presence of his two friends Derek rushed into the living room and strode towards the back wall. There was no sign of the black eyes or angular face of the thing that claimed to be Cindy. Just a whiff of her favourite perfume lingered.

'I don't understand,' he said half to himself.

'What don't you understand?' Jamie asked.

'She was here, Jamie, she was talking to me.'

'Who was?'

'Cindy.'

'What do you mean? She's dead, you do remember

35

that?' Jamie said.

'Yes, of course I do,' Derek spat back. 'But she was here, just now, talking to me. She wanted to give me a kiss. It was awful.'

'Derek, when did you last get some sleep?' Jamie asked quietly.

'I know what you're thinking. It's all in my head, but it isn't. She was here, it was awful, I couldn't move. I think she wanted to kill me.'

'She's dead,' Marco added, 'and you still need to tell the police about that.'

'Not now,' Jamie replied dismissively. 'I told you the police won't help.'

'It was real,' Derek insisted, turning around to face his two friends. 'I think we need to go and tell Mr Blaine about it.'

'That's why we're here Derek, Blaine's dead.'

'What do you mean?'

'It turns out he was some kind of evil monster, and the lycans have killed him.'

'Then who's in charge?'

'I don't know. I guess that Bob fellow is.'

'He's an idiot,' Derek said with a sigh.

'I don't know him well enough to comment.' Jamie said.

'Should we be talking about all this in front of him,' Derek asked, pointing at Marco.

'He's fine. He's one of us now. Got attacked by a strange water creature the other day. I took him over to the shop to tell Blaine, that's how I found out what's happened.'

'Well, whoever is in charge, we need to go and tell them about this. I think they'll want to know. That wasn't Cindy. I could be in all sorts of danger if they can get into my house and threaten me like that. I need help.' Derek shuddered at the thought of being so exposed.

'If you're sure?' Jamie said.

'Of course I am,' Derek replied with conviction, picking up his fallen sign and striding towards the front door. 'Besides, I need to get out of here.'

GOING UNDERGROUND

Lewis sighed loudly. Bob and Calder looked at him, but said nothing, as they made their way down the stairs. Like Charlie, Lewis was an unremarkable looking character for someone who was supposed to be a blood royal. He was of average height, had a slim build and a crown of messy brown hair he never combed. The only remarkable thing about his forgettable face was the ice blue eyes that stared out at you. Those you remembered. He felt nervous about being back at Victoria Station so quickly after the last visit. It didn't go well. Bob assured him that he was safe now that he'd turned, and the power coursing through him did feel reassuring. But he still felt his heart race inside his chest when he caught sight of the mass of magical creatures milling around the platform.

'Come on, it'll be fine,' Bob said, patting him reassuringly on the shoulder. He was still dressed in the green jacket and red trousers he'd put on to attend the funeral. It was unusual to see him in anything other than his combat fatigues and jacket and the bright outfit made him look out of place in the dank sewer.

'I seem to remember you saying it'll be fine last time,'

Lewis replied.

'I was lying last time.'

'What's to say you're not lying now?'

'The blood power coursing through your veins, come on.'

'What about me?' Calder asked.

'You'll be fine, you're half magical anyway.'

They entered the large cavern that made up the old station and made their way through the throng without incident. Lewis was struck once again by how un-station like the area appeared. The platform was three times as big as any he'd seen in a normal station, and the space was so cavernous you couldn't see the roof. The odd creature did try to get to Lewis, as they made their way to The Gatherers lair, but Bob pushed them away and they raced through the crowd quickly. Lewis was surprised to see a few of the creatures move aside as he passed. One even tugged its forelock. Before he knew it, they were standing in front of the entrance to The Gatherer's cave. The strange gatekeeper was seated in the same position as before, but Gral was standing over him this time, whispering into his ear.

'The Prince approaches,' the seated man intoned, bowing his head.

'Where's my money?' Gral spat at Bob as they approached.

'Here,' he replied, throwing something at the creature.

Gral deftly caught the flash of red that streaked across the space between them and stared down into his palm.

'This will do,' he said gruffly, then turned on his heels and disappeared into the crowd.

'What did you give him?' Lewis asked.

'Only what I owed. We need to see The Gatherer,' Bob said, ignoring Lewis's stare.

'The Prince of the Blood may see The Gatherer when he chooses, but payment is required,' the man replied, scribbling furiously in the little book he held in his hand.

'Thought so, this should be enough,' Bob replied, throwing a gold coin at him.

The man caught it without looking up, and popped it into his mouth. After a few moments of chewing he nodded and pointed behind him.

'Nice to do business with you.' Bob said.

'Where did you get the money from; I thought you were broke?' Lewis asked.

'Where do you think?'

'The shop?'

'Yep. Blaine doesn't need it anymore.'

'I didn't know it was yours to take.'

'Finder's keepers, mate.'

'It appears so,' Lewis said with a shake of his head.

Calder walked up to the gatekeeper and dropped a coin into his hand. 'I have questions, too,' he said when Lewis looked at him quizzically.

They entered the cave and Lewis was struck by the stench of rotting garbage once again. He gagged and put his hand over his nose. 'I would have thought he'd have cleaned up a bit by now.'

Bob just laughed and shook his head. The Gatherer was seated in the same place as before. A mountain of garbage surrounding him. His greasy locks still hiding most of his face and the stench of rotting food still emanating from him like heat.

'We have come for an audience,' Bob intoned, bowing his head.

'I see the prince has grown into his kingdom,' the creature whispered.

'I've found my blood power, if that's what you mean?'

'I also see you have chosen sides.'

'It wasn't that hard. Blaine was a demon after all. As are you, Baal.'

A half hidden smile spread across the creature's face. 'You have been doing your research. I know why you have come, my Prince. You seek a way to prevent my brothers from crossing over and to kill them if they do. You seek information on swords and perhaps portals too?'

'Swords or anything else that can kill them.'

39

'They must be on this plane for you to kill them. You sent my brothers back with your power, but you did not kill them. They know how powerful you are now and will not take you for granted next time.'

'So, we can kill them?'

'Yes.'

'What things can kill them?'

'I think you already know how.'

'Swords?'

'Yes. Our link to this world is anchored through battle swords, but it makes us vulnerable. We have to put our spirit into the steel. That means it's the only thing in the universe that can kill us. There are nine, one for each of us.'

'Where do the portals come into this?' Calder asked.

'You cannot go to hell and kill my brothers, so you must wait until they enter this realm. There are a number of ways they can come through, but the portals are the easiest.'

'How may portals are there?'

'You ask a lot of questions for the price you have paid, my Prince,' the demon responded with another smile.

'I thought I could?'

'At a cost.'

Bob reached into his pocket and took out another gold coin. 'Will this do?'

'Yes. Pay my keeper on your way out. There are nine, one for each of us.'

'Convenient.' Lewis said.

'But do not ask me where they are. I can only reveal so much.'

'OK, but how do we start looking for them?' Lewis asked.

'I suspect help will come from an unusual source. You must be patient.'

'OK, what about the swords, how do we find them?' Bob asked.

'That you will have to figure out for yourself. This audience is at an end, good day.'

'Wait,' Calder said. 'I've paid my coin. I have questions.'

40

'Ask away.'

'Where's Mono?'

'Ah, you seek revenge, Mr Rouge?'

'Yes.'

'I cannot help you kill another creature.'

'You were doing a good job of it telling us how to kill your brothers,' Lewis said sarcastically.

'That is my oath,' The Gatherer said, ignoring Lewis. 'That is why I could not help Bob when he asked me where The Dark Man was hiding. But know this, his master has returned, and he will seek you out in due course.'

'What! You mean The Dark Man has returned?' Lewis gasped.

'Yes, he is now on this plane of existence. You need to prepare yourselves. He is coming and he will not underestimate you as he did last time.'

'How did he get back so quickly?'

'Because Blaine is dead,' Calder said coldly.

'Yes. Asmodeus helped keep the doors shut. That magic is fading now he is back in hell.'

'So, the others can come through now?' Lewis asked.

The Gatherer only smiled in reply. 'Good day to you all.'

They exited the cavern and walked gasping into the semi-clean air of the station.

'He really needs to do something about that hygiene problem,' Bob said.

'So we need to find the swords so we can kill them when they come through?' Lewis asked, taking Bob by the arm and pulling him close.

'Yes, and the portals. If we can find them, we have a chance of killing the demons when they try and get through.'

'That's no good, we can't kill them without the swords, and what do we do about The Dark Man?'

'Nothing for now.'

'We need to find both,' Calder interjected. 'We find the portals, and once they're here we kill them with the swords and have done with the whole lot of them.'

'Easier said than done. There are nine portals and probably nine swords too, none of which we have. I bet they need the swords to get though the portals too. If we have the swords, they can't get through.'

'If you're right about that, The Dark Man must already have his sword if he's come through a portal,' Lewis said.

'Probably, but we can't be sure, and our smelly friend's not saying.' Bob replied. 'As for the swords, we know that The Gatherer has one, thanks to Calder, and probably The Dark Man too, if Lewis is right. I bet The Gatherer is sitting on a portal too. That's why he never moves from his smelly hovel. I bet he has his own sword in there as well, which means he has two.'

'We still have to find seven other portals and retrieve all nine swords.' Lewis said.

'It's better than nothing. Besides, let's think about this logically. The portals aren't going to be anywhere public. They'll be ancient places and probably hidden too.'

So, who do we know who can find hidden old places?' Lewis asked.

'Derek,' they said in unison.

JILLIAN LIGHTFOOT

The rain fell in a steady drizzle, soaking the ground and making the pavements shine. Little moved, apart from the odd worker trying to find their way home and those that had already found one out on the streets.

Jillian Lightfoot moved through the sodden streets in deep contemplation. Her white jacket and peroxide blonde hair making her stand out amongst the grey jackets and black umbrellas. She didn't like what she's been asked to do, and she liked how she was supposed to do it even less. How could they ask this of her, and here of all places? She hated Glasgow. It held particularly difficult memories for her. It had been a long time since she'd last visited the city, but the pain was still fresh. She could still hear the screams and smell the copper tang of fresh blood. The feelings of horror and disbelief still lingered. This surprised her, she was used to horror in her line of work. But it's different when those who die are the ones you love. Then the pain takes on a whole other meaning. She wore it now like a shroud, reluctant to shrug it off, unwilling to let them go. Her boss had told her many times that to heal you had to forgive, but Jillian couldn't forgive, or forget. She'd avoided the scene of the crime when she first arrived, but her wanderings through the damp city eventually took her back to it. Now here she was standing at the foot of the Tolbooth, staring up into the dark sky beyond.

'They suffered in those days,' a voice whispered from behind her.

'It was a nasty time.'

'But the crowd seemed to revel in the pain and feed off the blood and gore.'

'Not much of that when you're hanging someone. Why are you here, Gideon?'

'To see how you are.'

'You haven't concerned yourself with my wellbeing for a millennium, why worry now?'

'We are approaching the end game, and she wishes to ensure you complete your task.'

'I thought she knew all things? If so, then she will surely know the outcome of this?'

'Humans and their strange beliefs,' Gideon replied with a shake of his head.

'We are nothing without them.'

'We are less, that is true, but we are creatures of the sky, we can do without their love.'

'I can't,' Jillian whispered half to herself.

'No. That is why you are well suited to this; your empathy serves you well.'

'You can tell her it will be done, have no fear.'

'I don't, you seem to be the one that specialises in that.'

'And a great many other things that you lack.'

'You have special talents, that is true, but never forget who you are or where you have come from.'

'How could I, when you are always here to remind me?'

'I will always be here for that, never fear.' He bowed his head before she could reply and disappeared back into the gloom.

Jillian turned her attention back to the Tolbooth, its looming presence hanging heavy over her mood. 'Why wasn't I able to stop them?' she whispered to herself. She could see the baying crowd in her mind's eye, all there in anticipation of blood. They had brought the victims out one at a time and displayed them in front of the jeering multitude, announcing to the throng the many crimes that they had been found guilty of. When this was complete, they had been taken up and into the Tolbooth, ascending the dreaded steps with heavy feet. Halfway up they reached the killing floor, where a noose had been placed around their necks. A door was opened up at the bottom, so the crowd could view the bodies as they reached the end of the rope. Then the trap door had been released and they'd been sent to hell.

Jillian shuddered at the memory. The remembered sound as neck after neck broke sent a shiver down her spine. The feelings of pain and loss were as fresh as if it had happened yesterday. It had been the one time in her long existence when she had let someone down. She couldn't have helped them, no matter how hard she tried. Their fate had been set and God had done nothing to intervene. Just one of the many reasons why she still wasn't talking to her.

Jillian pulled her coat close around her and pondered her latest task. She was to find the so called 'Prince of the Blood' and guide him as best she could. A simple task you would have thought, only she was supposed to guide him where he didn't want to go. 'So we betray them once again; how many more times will you ignore their love?' she said to herself.

The Tolbooth seemed to shudder in response, before settling back down to its eternal contemplation.

THE SHOP OF
INTERESTING
DISCOVERIES

For once, the shop was warm and cosy, things it had rarely been in its long life. The warmth came from a large fire that had been lit, and the camaraderie of the group of lycans who sat around laughing and joking. Although the battle had been won six weeks ago, they were still basking in the glory of their victory, sharing war stories and comparing scars. Charlie, Lewis and Bob, sat away from the rest, deep in conversation. Midgy sat slightly apart from them, looking very uncomfortable in his new surroundings.

Fiona sat next to Guils and laughed. They had faced death together many times before, but the battle of the two armies, as the victory over The Dark Man and his minions was being called, had been a close one. Fiona had been convinced that she was going to die and had been ready for it. The fact that she was now sitting in a warm room, swopping battle stories, still made her feel giddy.

'So, what are you going to do now that Blaine's gone?'

Guils asked for the thousandth time.

'Like I said before, I don't know. We're busy mopping up the rest of the werewolves anyway. Why do you ask?'

'We were fighting for the bad guys, Fi. I don't know about you, but I'm not sure I can carry on now I know that? I've only stayed as long as I have because of you and Bob.'

'We didn't know he was one of the bad guys, and we did a lot of good. We killed dozens of werewolves, and we've just sent him and that other demon back to hell. That doesn't sound like working for the bad guys to me.'

'Yeah, but what about all those years with him running the show? How many innocent lycans got killed because of him? And we just let it happen.'

'We didn't know, G. If we did, we would have stopped him, you know that.'

'I just don't know,' she said with a sigh. 'I feel like someone should have seen something. I mean, he'd been at it for years.'

'Hiding in plain sight. He was good at it, he had us all fooled.'

'Except Charlie,' Guils said.

'Yeah, except her. She's a clever one, I think she'll go far,' Fiona replied, laughing. 'Besides,' she added. 'That's what we do now. We protect the Prince and Princess. I figure there's a war coming and they're going to need all the help they can get.'

'You're not wrong,' Bob said from the other side of the room. He'd put on his normal attire of combat trousers and jacket, since returning from the station. They gave him the air of command, or at least he thought they did. Bob was the oldest lycan in the crew. He'd been in more battles than anyone alive and had the battle scars to prove it. A broken nose dominated the middle of his face. It sat below soft brown eyes and just above a mouth that was often set into a smirk.

'Listen up,' he shouted across the general hum of lycans all talking at once. 'We have a job to do, and I need your full attention. Blaine has gone.' There was a general shout of approval at that. 'But he's not dead. We sent him back to hell, but we now know he has a way of getting back to our world. We need to stop him, and all the others.'

'What others?' Fiona asked.

'Remember he has eight other brothers, all demons like him. Calder found that out when he visited The Gatherer to bargain for information by selling him Blaine's sword.'

'Oh yeah, I remember Blaine's face when he told him that,' Fi said with a smile.

'As best we can tell, most are in hell, where they belong. But it won't stay like that. There are portals into this world, and we know they can use them, and there are swords too. They're the only way we can kill the demons, so here's the deal; we need to find those portals and the swords.' Bob said.

'How do we do that?' Fiona asked.

'I'm coming to that' Bob replied.

'What if they get through before we find the portals?' she added.

'Then we're in trouble, so let's make sure that doesn't happen.' Bob said.

'That's not everything though, is it, Bob?' Guils asked.

'No. We don't know where all the portals or swords are, we need to find them first, because the demon's minions need the swords too. They're the main way of getting through the portals and the only thing that can kill them. So, it's a race to find the swords before the demons do.'

'So are we searching for swords or portals, I'm confused?' Fiona asked.

'Both, that's the problem. We need to split our forces. Some need to look for the portals, and some need to look for the swords,' Bob replied.

'What's the point of finding the portals if we don't have the swords? You said we can't kill them without the swords,' Fiona said.

'If we can find the portals, then we are ready for when we find the swords. Like I said, we need to find both as quickly as we can.'

'Hang on, what do we do if we find a portal and a demon is already there and they have a sword too?' someone asked from the back.

'One thing at a time, I can't consider everything.'

'We fight,' Lewis said. He'd been standing next to Bob, trying to work out how to get Blaine's sword back from The Gatherer, and probably his own as well, and had only been half listening to the conversation.

'And die,' Guils said.

'Yes, that's what soldiers do,' Lewis replied. 'But this time, I'll be there.'

'So will I,' Charlie said, 'I'll look for the portals, Lewis can look for the swords.'

Lewis nodded his agreement. 'Only problem is I've no idea where to start. The Gatherer was no help, so we need to figure this out on our own.'

'I know how to find the portals,' a voice said from the doorway. Everyone turned as one and stared at Derek as he walked into the shop accompanied by Marco.

'How?' Lewis asked.

'With this,' Derek replied, holding up the old railway sign he had brought with him. 'This is a sign from the old St Enoch's Railway Station, it closed in 1966. I've got loads but this is my favourite. There's something odd about it, something that's always puzzled me, until now. No matter how much research I did, I couldn't find out why the sign had a small pentagram embossed on the bottom right-hand corner. At first I thought it was a mistake, that something had gone wrong in the manufacturing process. But the more I looked, the more I realised that it couldn't have been an error. It was far too intricate to be anything other than deliberate. I've looked at thousands of different railway signs and seen nothing like this. Up until recently, I put it down to someone having a laugh or trying to say something obscure on the sign. I've just I heard what you said, and now everything make sense. It's the symbol for demon, the sign that shows there's a portal at that station. I came here for help, I think someone is trying to kill me and now I think it's a demon. If we can use the signs to find the portals, maybe we can close them and I'll be safe.'

Bob walked towards Derek and gently took the sign out of his hands. He stared at it for a long time, then let out a sigh. 'It makes sense. It's an easy way for any of their followers to find their way to the portals.'

'The other demons have followers?' Charlie asked.

'Of course. The world is made up of some very stupid people.'

'A lot of them in this room,' Derek said under his breath.

'Have you seen this symbol on any more signs?' Bob asked him.

'Yes, on one more, that makes me think all the portals will be at railway stations. They're busy places where people don't notice odd things and, even better if you're trying to hide something, they become abandoned and everyone forgets about them. I have the other sign back at my house and that's from an abandoned station too.'

'Where's the sign for?' Lewis asked.

'Creagan Station. It was abandoned long ago.'

'So, we have our first two portals,' Bob said with a smile.

'Hold on, there's no way we can be sure that's what the symbol means,' Lewis said.

'True,' Bob replied with a nod. 'There's only one way to find out.'

'I guess I'm going hunting in an abandoned station, what fun.' Charlie said through thin lips. 'I'll take Midgy with me, he could do with the run out.' Midgy nodded next to her and shifted uncomfortably as everyone stared at him.

'No problem, but you'll need to take more than him, take Fi, Guils and Derek as well.' Bob said.

Charlie nodded in response.

'Why don't we split our forces?' Bob asked. 'I can go to this Creagan place, and you can go to St Enoch's?'

'Fine with me,' she replied.

'That just leaves me and the swords. How the hell do we find them? Lewis said.

'Erm, I think we can help with that too,' a voice said from behind Derek. All eyes turned to Marco, who squirmed uncomfortably.

'How can you help?' Bob asked.

'Swords are my kind of thing, my dad used to collect them. It's how I got into antiques and learned about Abandoned Glasgow, and all that. My dad has a decent collection of them and knows everything about where to find others. Who owns them, what's up for sale, that kind of thing.'

'Somehow I don't think these swords will come up at auction,' Lewis said with a smile.

'That's where you're wrong,' Marco replied, bright eyed and smiling in return. 'I think I know exactly the kind of swords you're looking for. They have to be the same as the railway signs. I've heard about ones that have the pentagram embossed onto them. That's a unique design for an original sword and definitely draws a collector's attention.'

'So that's a thing? We can find them that way?'

'Some at least. I know of at least three that are held by a local collector.'

'That's brilliant!' Lewis said. 'Let's go and make him a house call.'

'He's a she, and she doesn't like visitors.'

'Oh, don't worry, she'll love me,' Lewis replied with a grin. Before leaving he gently took Charlie by the arm and led her into the back room. 'The Dark Man is back,' he said softly, so he wouldn't be overheard.'

'What!' Charlie said, with a start.

'Keep your voice down, we don't want everyone else to know just yet. We need to focus on the swords and the portals.'

'But if he's back, we're all in danger.'

'Nothing new there, then,' Lewis said with a chuckle.

'I suppose not,' Charlie said with a sigh. 'I thought we'd seen the back of that one.'

'Yeah, so did I. Don't worry, we'll get him, and this time he's not coming back. Are you OK?'

'What do you mean?'

'You've just buried your gran; you don't need to go on this mission if you don't want to.'

'It's a mission, now, is it?' Charlie said laughing,' I'll be fine; besides I'd like to keep busy.'

Lewis nodded and turned back to Marco, 'OK, let's get going.'

THE HOUSE ON OLD
BOTHWELL ROAD

The house had been there since the seventeenth century. Originally a summer house for the landed gentry, it had long since fallen into disrepair. Ivy grew over its walls, covering most of the large windows and wrapping around the roof and chimney pots. The garden, once an immaculate lawn where croquet had been played on hot summer days, was now choked with weeds and large bushes. The flower beds had all died, and the mini maze had grown into a tangle of bushes and weeds. The only part of the house now visible to the outside world was the large red door facing the street at the end of a winding broken path. It had been kept clear of weeds and ivy, and a large sign was planted in front, loudly proclaiming that trespassers would be eaten.

Lewis stood in front of the door and laughed. 'That's original,' he said.

'Probably true as well,' Marco replied, shifting uneasily from one foot to the other. 'OK, so I've got you to the door, I think it's really over to you now.'

'What's your worry? You told me she was just an old

lady.'

'A mental old lady.'

'I'm sure that's not true.'

'Oh, it's true. I heard she killed her son when she caught him playing with her swords. That's mental if you ask me.'

'Probably just a story, like you say. Either way, I need you to introduce me, she knows you.'

'She knows my dad.'

'Same thing. Come on, we won't be long, this is really important.'

Marco sighed. Although he was new to this world, he already understood enough to know that Lewis was important, and finding the swords equally so.

'OK, let's go,' he said, knocking on the door and quickly stepping back.

'Has the door got an electric current running through it?' Lewis asked, laughing.

Marco shrugged and took another step back.

They waited in silence for a minute, then the door opened with a long slow creaking sound that seemed to Lewis like a cry for help.

'Who is it? What do you want?'

'Mrs Winters, it's Marco, Joe's son.'

'Who? I don't know any Marco.' The door opened a little more to reveal a wizened old woman, stooped with age. Her hair was a shocking white and her small body was enveloped in a grey shawl that was probably as old as the house.

'Joe Dent, you know Joe, he bought that lovely Damascene sword off you last year.'

The old woman peered at him through watery eyes. 'So, what do you want?'

'We want to talk to you about demons,' Lewis said, stepping forward.

The old woman took in a sharp breath, gripping the edge of the door tightly. She stared at Lewis for an age, then nodded slowly.

'You better come in, then,' she said, opening the door

wide.

'Thank you, Mrs Winters,' Lewis said, smiling at Marco as they entered the house. 'Easy.'

'Yeah, we'll see.'

The interior hallway was dark and smelt of cigarettes and furniture polish. It was lit by a pale bulb, whose light seemed to die as soon as it hit the walls. Dark oak doors stood off at intervals on both sides, and a black door stood at the very end. The old woman shuffled down the hallway and opened the first door on her right. She entered the room and gestured for them to follow.

The room was full of weaponry. The walls were crammed with swords of every kind; broadswords, cutlasses, scimitars, claymores and katanas were just a few that Lewis could recognise. They were displayed alongside axes, maces, pikes and shields. A glass cabinet along one wall displayed the largest broadsword Lewis had ever seen, and a spear hung precariously from the ceiling.

'Sit down,' the old woman ordered as she shuffled into an armchair.

They both sat down on a large leather two seater, that sighed as they sank into it.

'So, you want to talk about demons?' the old woman asked.

'Well, we really want to talk to you about swords,' Marco replied.

'Demon swords,' Lewis added.

'I thought you might. You come to someone you know collects swords, but you ask about demons. Stands to reason. Are you who I think you are?' she asked Lewis, over a hard stare.

'That depends; who do you think I am?'

'The Prince of the Blood.'

'Yes.'

'Then I know why you're here. You want my demon swords.'

Lewis nodded slowly in response.

'Well, you can't have them,' the old women said,

snuggling further into her shawl.

'Not even if the fate of the world depends on it?'

'Not even then.'

'Not even if we ask nicely?' Lewis asked.

'Especially if you ask nicely.'

'Tell me about them.'

'They're swords, what else is there to tell?'

'But what makes them demon swords?'

'They are not of this earth. They were created in the forges of hell, the hottest in existence. They were created out of the screams of the demon's victims. They are the most evil artefact in the universe, and I have three of them.'

'How do we tell them apart from any other sword?' Lewis asked.

'The markings, of course. Without them they look as ordinary as any other weapon. Each sword has a pentagram and bears the mark of its maker. The mark of the demon. It's how you tell them apart.'

'How on earth did you find three of them?' Marco asked.

'I collect swords. They come to my attention in many ways.'

'But that's not quite true, is it?' Lewis said, moving to the edge of his seat. 'You need to know about them first, and then you need to find them. Most collectors would dismiss them as an urban myth, but you've found three of them. That's quite a feat.

'I had a bit of luck; every collector needs that.'

'Oh, I bet you did. Tell me, which one did you kill first?'

'What?'

'You took them, didn't you? Probably as you killed each of your brothers.'

'Oh, they're not dead,' the old woman replied with a smile. 'They're just back in hell, where they belong.'

'Who is?' Marco asked.

'Keep up, mate,' Lewis murmured as he rose from his seat. 'So, which one are you?'

'As if I'd tell a human my name!' the woman snapped

back, spittle and black bile tumbling from her mouth.

'I'm not a human, you will tell me, demon, just before I send you back to hell.'

The old woman launched herself at Lewis. No longer a shuffling old lady, she was now a lightening quick monster. Lewis has been ready for her. He changed in a heartbeat and snapped his massive jaws towards her scrawny neck, missing by inches. They collided in the middle of the room, the thunder clap smashing glass cabinets and sending Marco tumbling to the floor.

The duo rolled over the old woman's armchair and disappeared from view. Marco dusted himself off and staggered towards the opposite side of the room from the combatants, while he had the chance.

For a few moments, nothing happened, then the old woman launched herself into the air and clung to the ceiling, hissing and spitting at the lycan, as it appeared from behind the arm chair. He growled at the woman clinging to the ceiling, then launched himself at her, gripping onto her ankle and dragging her down to the floor. She let out a roar of agony and began beating at his head. He shook her ankle between his teeth, then leaped over the top of her sprawling body, changing back into Lewis as he did. Without a second's pause, Lewis plunged his hand into the old woman's chest and gripped her heart. She let out a moan and gripped his arm with her weathered hands.

'Oh, my God, Lewis, what are you doing! You're going to kill her,' Marco shouted from the corner of the room.

'She's a demon you idiot, and yes, I'm going to kill it,' Lewis hissed, squeezing the heart between his fingers. 'Tell me your name.'

'No,' the demon moaned.

'Tell me your name, and I'll make it quick.'

'My brothers will avenge me.'

'The ones you sent back to hell? I don't think they will. I think they'll be glad to see you, so they can inflict as much pain on you as you have on them. But before you go, I'll make your last moments on this earth a true agony, unless you tell me your name.'

The demon looked at Lewis with hatred in its eyes. It huffed and puffed, writhing around as it tried to get out of Lewis's death grip, but he had a tight hold on the withered heart and began to squeeze harder.

The demon let out another roar of agony then spluttered out its name, 'Amoyman, I am Amoyman.'

Lewis nodded and squeezed the life out of the creature's heart. He jumped back as the body turned black and began to hiss and spit, before being engulfed in blue flame.

'What the hell was that?' Marco asked.

'Hell is about right; it was a demon.'

'How did you know it wasn't human?'

'The smell. I can recognise it now. I knew as soon as we walked into the house. Come on, we have three swords to find, maybe even four if this demon had possession of its own one too. It's a pity I couldn't find the swords first, then I might have been able to kill it, instead of just sending it back to hell.'

Marco stood on shaky legs then nodded. 'I thought that Blaine was a demon. Why couldn't you smell him?'

'Because he was extra good at hiding in plain sight.'

'I don't see anything that looks like the swords we're looking for in this room.'

'No, it wouldn't let us into the same room as its prize possessions. They'll be hidden somewhere.'

They began to scout out the old house, and quickly found the decayed body of an old man.

'That must have been her husband,' Marco speculated.

'Yep. The thing didn't want to arouse suspicion by getting rid of the body somewhere else, so it must have decided to keep it in the house. Disgusting.'

They continued their search and finally found three swords wrapped in a blanket at the bottom of a wardrobe in one of the bedrooms. Lewis carefully unwrapped the swords and stared at them. They glowed a dull gold, and Marco was sure he could hear a faint hum coming off them. Lewis picked one up and hefted it in his hand. It cut through the air, leaving a faint line in its wake. He noticed a small pentagram symbol on the cross guard, and what could only be the demon's name imprinted on the pommel.

'It just feels wrong,' he said after a few more moments of quiet. The longer he held it the more he felt he wanted to stare at it, and marvel at its golden form.

'As long as you keep it out of the hands of the demons, I don't think that matters.'

'The demon didn't hide them very well.'

'I bet it thought that hiding itself away in this big old house was probably enough.'

'Yeah, I guess.'

Lewis put the sword down, reluctantly, and picked up another one. It looked and felt the same. The only difference seemed to be the name on the pommel, but they couldn't be sure until they got it translated.

'Why did you want to know its name?' Marco asked quietly.

'So I know who I've sent back to hell, and who I still need to find.'

'So you know all their names, then?'

'No, not yet, but I'm going to find out. OK, we better get these back to the shop.'

'No, not me, I'm done. I brought you here, like you asked, I'll leave you to the rest of it.'

'Fair enough mate, but remember, they won't leave you alone just because you don't want to be involved anymore.'

'I'll take my chances,' Marco replied, his face set.

'OK, but don't come running to me when they search you out, you're on your own.'

Marco swallowed at the thought and helped him wrap the swords.

ST ENOCH'S STATION

Charlie sighed as her foot pressed down on something soft and squishy. She was in a dark tunnel, and she hated it. She didn't know why they hadn't used a magical seed to call the chute like last time. The magical underground transport would have gotten them to the station much quicker. The small space they were walking down meant she kept knocking into Guils and Fi as they walked next to her and Derek, walking just in front, had covered himself in so much cheap aftershave, that the smell clogged Charlie's nostrils and made her feel sick. Midgy, the fifth member of their little group, stayed out of the way at the back, clearly trying to keep away from Derek's pungent smell. Derek himself was adamant this was the quickest way down to the old station, he didn't know anything about magical transportation.

She thought back over the conversation they'd had before they left the shop and wondered why she'd volunteered to search for the portals. At first she thought she'd be out in the fresh air, helping to take her mind of her gran, and maybe even finding a portal, after a nice walk in the woods. Going back down into the underground below Glasgow wasn't what she had in mind.

'It's not too far down this tunnel now,' Derek said excitedly.

'Can't wait,' Charlie replied.

'Cheer up, girly. This is a great adventure.'

'It will bc if you call me girly one more time,' Charlie warned him.

'My apologies, would you prefer Princess?' Derek asked, with a chuckle.

'Just Charlie will do.'

'OK, Just Charlie, we're here,' he said grandly.

They exited the tunnel and walked up onto a platform that stretched away into the gloom. It was covered in rotting litter, and rats scurried about around the edge of their torches. The air smelt of death and despair, and Charlie was convinced something had died down here recently.

'This is lovely,' Fi said sarcastically.

'Yeah, a great place for a first date,' Guils added.

'Well, it's an old abandoned station, what do you expect?' Derek asked with a shrug.

'OK, so what are we looking for?' Fi asked.

'Any signs of werewolves? I think they may be attracted to where their masters might appear.'

'I don't smell them,' Midgy said.

'No, but there's something else. I can't quite put my finger on it.'

'I can,' Fi said from further down the platform. She was standing over a crumpled form, her torch covering it in a pool of stark light.

Charlie gasped when she reached the spot. 'What's that? It looks like a devil.'

'No, it's a faun. Totally harmless. Why would anyone want to kill it?' Guils said to herself.

'They've not just killed it, they've ripped it apart. Those are werewolf bites,' Charlie said as she crouched down to look at the dead creature more closely.

'So why can't we smell them if werewolves have been here?' Midgy asked.

'The thing's been dead a while and it's filled the place

with its stench. Do werewolves kill other magical creatures?' Charlie asked.

'Yeah, they've been known to, but only when they're defending their master. Otherwise, they just ignore them.' Fi replied.

'There's our answer, then; a demon's come through here. I bet the faun just happened along at the wrong time.' Charlie said.

'There's a wound on its neck that looks like it was made by a sword,' Derek said, pointing towards the dead creature.

'Yep, it looks like it,' Charlie agreed.

'So they've been here. and they had a sword. I'm guessing another demon came through a portal?' Fi said.

Charlie nodded in reply. 'At least we know this is definitely a portal.'

'Yes, after the horse has bolted,' Derek said.

'It's a start.' Charlie said with a shrug.

'Not a very good one.' Derek replied.

'What's that over there?' Guils asked.

Charlie walked over to the spot Guils was pointing at and looked down at a dark stain on the platform floor.

'Looks like something else was killed here too, but whatever it was has been taken away.'

'There're a few other stains over here too,' Midgy said.

'This is carnage,' Fi whispered. 'So, what do we do now? Do we need to guard the place in case they come back?'

'No, I don't think so. Why would they come back now that the demon's through?' Charlie said.

'So why are we looking for these places then?' Fi asked.

'To find them all first and see if there's been any activity. We need as much info as we can, so we can plan our next move.' Charlie replied.

'But what *is* our next move?' Guils asked.

Charlie was stumped for a moment. She really didn't know what their next move was. She was so fixed on finding the portals, she really had no idea what they were going to do now they'd found one, other than go back to the shop for a cup of tea.

'Derek, how many members does your group have?'

'Ten, why?'

'Do they fancy doing a bit of surveillance?'

'What do you mean?' Derek asked her.

'We need to know if anyone comes back here, but we need to keep searching for the other portals. How about your members keep watch at each portal once we find it and then report back anything suspicious they see? That way we can react as soon as the werewolves show their faces.'

'Or the demons,' Derek said excitedly.

'Yep, them too.'

'I'm sure they'd all be thrilled. I know just the fellow to keep watch here too,' Derek said with a wide grin.'

HOMECOMING

Scarlett sighed. She hadn't been home in weeks and wondered what kind of reception she would get. If her house was anything to go by, it wouldn't be a warm one. The windows were boarded up and it was clear no one had been near the place in weeks. She wondered how Bob had managed to keep her son out of the authorities' hands while she'd been away, and their house had clearly been abandoned. She reviewed her decision to disappear for the millionth time and cursed Bob once again. She hated being away from her son, hated the fact she had left him without even saying goodbye. She'd been convinced by Bob that it was the right thing to do, that searching for the newly returned demon was the only thing she could do to protect him. That hadn't worked out well, she hadn't found the demon, and then she'd discovered that there had been one right under her nose all along. She cursed Bob for that too. She had no idea what pain her son had been through, and it hurt her to think that he'd had to go through it alone, without his mum to guide and support him, as she should have done when he had come into his power. If she'd realised he was that close, she would have never left, despite what Bob and

Blaine had said. She'd heard through the grapevine that Doris, Charlie's gran, had died too and she felt another stab of remorse. She should have been here to support her old friend, and her grandchild, in their hour of need.

'What good are you, really?' she asked herself once again. 'You weren't here when they needed you, you were off chasing a ghost.'

'You're here now, that's what counts,' a voice answered her from behind.

Scarlett whirled around with a start. 'Oh, my God, you gave me a hell of a fright!'

'Hell, really?' Calder said, raising an eyebrow.

'You know what I mean. Why are you here?'

'I'm the welcoming committee, didn't Bob say?'

'No, he didn't, I thought I was slipping back in unnoticed.'

'No need for that now Blaine's gone.'

'There's always a need. He may be gone from this earth, but he can still come back, and I'm not only talking about him.'

'Yeah, we have lots of enemies.'

'We certainly do. Glad to see you finally decided to join the good guys. How did you know where I'd be; I only told Bob I was coming back?'

'I figured this would be the first place you'd visit, and I've been here lots lately.'

'Oh, really, why?'

'Just looking out for the boy,' Calder replied nervously.

'What happened here?'

'Werewolves,' he replied with a shrug.

'That figures. What about the police? Didn't they get suspicious when my house was trashed and I didn't turn up?'

'Nah, Bob took care of them, and the social workers as well. They stuck their noses in when you didn't show, worried about Lewis and lack of parental care apparently, even though he's turned seventeen and doesn't need it anymore. Come on, I need to take you back to the shop. Lewis will be there.'

'OK,' Scarlett replied, nodding nervously. 'How is he?'

'Oh, he's fine, he's our saviour now.'

'Yeah, I'd heard that.'

'He's really come into his own. His power is immense. He sent both demons back with nothing but his power, and Charlie's as well. They make a real team.'

'I bet. So, he sent them back to hell, but that didn't kill them?'

'No, he didn't have any of the swords.'

'What swords?'

'We learnt later that the only way to truly kill a demon is to use his own sword on him. Each one has a special sword that tethers them to this world, strike them down with it and they are dead.'

'That sounds easy,' Scarlett laughed.

'Yes, well, now we know, we can look for them.'

'Is that what they're doing, looking for the swords?'

'Amongst other things. I'm sure Lewis will fill you in when we get to the shop.'

'If he's speaking to me. How is he really, Calder?'

'Like I said, he's fine. He's handled it all better than anyone expected. He's taken to it like a duck to water.'

'And Charlie? Losing her gran must have been awful for her?'

'She's fine too. She didn't find it as easy at first, but she's getting there.'

'What about you? I didn't think you were this committed to the cause.'

'Another long story,' Calder said hastily, 'I'll fill you in later. Come on, we need to get going.'

They walked towards Calder's car and got in, without another word. Calder started the engine and they began to trundle down the road.

'Why the shop?' Scarlett asked.

'It seemed like the best place once Blaine had gone. Sort of like the spoils of war.'

'Blaine,' Scarlett said, shaking her head.

'Yeah, it looks like you and Bob had his number before

anyone else did.'

'It was a feeling more than anything. We didn't have any evidence of what he was doing, it's just that he didn't seem right. It took us an age to sense something was wrong.'

'Is that why you left?'

'No, I needed to go on a personal mission. I'm just sorry it had to be now, but I had no choice. It meant I wasn't here when he needed me.'

'Well, it all worked out in the end.'

'I'm not so sure, especially now you say Blaine isn't dead.'

'One step at a time.'

They didn't see the other car until the headlights filled the passenger side window. The two cars hit each other at speed, sending Calder's car hurling across the road and smashing into a hedgerow on the far side. The car's safety features saved Scarlett's life, but she was knocked unconscious and rattled around her seat like a rag doll, until the car stopped. Calder wasn't so lucky. He was left leaning over the steering wheel, blood pouring from numerous cuts. All was quiet after the impact, until the sound of shoes crackling over broken glass broke the silence. Mr Mono's grey eyes came level with Scarlett's unconscious face, a smile painfully spread across his metallic face.

'How nice to see you again, my dear,' he said. 'I know someone who's been dying to meet you.'

HEARTH AND HOME

Charlie sat down and let out a long sigh, they'd just returned to the shop after their trip to St Enoch's Station and she was tired. She'd spent the last few hours in Derek's company and was just about ready to throttle him. It wasn't so much his insulting comments about her age and gender, which were bad enough, but his general arrogance that got under her skin. He was an insufferable know-it-all. He droned on about the hidden treasures of Glasgow he'd accumulated, not to mention the extensive collection of nails he kept at home. She'd managed to tune out his constant drawl while they'd travelled back to the shop, but he grew louder as they entered the building and spied a new audience.

'Yes, you can really learn a lot about a city by the different types of nails they used in the buildings.'

Charlie saw several people shuffle out of the general vicinity when they saw Derek appear. Guils, Midgy and Fi disappeared as soon as they got back to the shop, too. She couldn't blame them; she'd disappear too if she could.

'OK!' she said, a little too loudly. 'Now we've found a portal and got your mates to stake it out, we really need to go and find the others. You said you had other signs at home?'

'Well, yes, we could use them,' Derek replied through thin lips. He hated being interrupted at the best of times, but particularly when it was an arrogant young female like this. 'They don't have symbols on them, but I don't think we need to look for a sign now.'

'Why not?'

'Because I believe there is a clear pattern here. We went to St Enoch's Station, and Bob has gone over to Creagan.'

'So?'

'Well, what do you think they have in common?'

'They're both stations?' Charlie replied with a shrug.

'No. They're both *abandoned* stations.' Derek paused for dramatic effect and was put out by Charlie's blank look. 'You really did hit the jackpot on this one. Getting the help of the one man who knows all about the abandoned stations of Scotland. I'm talking of myself, obviously.'

'Obviously,' Charlie replied slowly. 'How can you be so sure?'

'It's obvious. The portals have probably been in the same spots for centuries, but it's no coincidence that the ones we know about are in public places. That's where most people don't linger or ask questions, and they tend to be places built on older buildings. It also stands to reason that they are in smaller stations, not large central ones where they do a lot of digging and redesigning. A lot of those smaller stations have become abandoned over the years, so where better to focus our search?'

Charlie considered this for a moment. She remembered the abandoned zoo that The Dark Man had hidden in. She was reluctant to admit it, but it all made sense. 'Yeah, that makes sense. How many are there?'

'Quite a few, I think. I'll write them down and we can see which ones are closest and take a trip.'

Another trip with Derek didn't appeal all that much to Charlie, but needs must and all that.

'OK. Do you think there'll be a lot in and around Glasgow?'

'Some, but closures tended to be random, depending on demand, so they could be all over the place.'

'Lovely.'

Derek nodded and started to look for paper and a pen. Charlie took her opportunity and went into the back of the shop to get away from him. She spied Midgy, Guils and Fi there, each one hugging a steaming cup of tea.

'Say what you want about Blaine, he knew his teas,' Fi said.

'Any left?' Charlie asked.

'Yeah, help yourself,' Fi replied, nodding towards the tea pot in the middle of the table. 'Has anyone seen Curly lately?'

'Yep, he was going to tell Martine's mum about her dying at the battle, we finally tracked down where she lives, then he was going to search for werewolves,' Guils said.

'Oh, I don't envy him that one.' Fi shivered at the memory of Martine's death during the battle of the two armies. 'Where's his highness gone?'

'He's looking for a pen and paper. He thinks he knows where the other portals might be?' Charlie said.

'Really?' Guils asked, raising her eyebrows.

'Yep, and it actually makes sense. He thinks they're all in abandoned railway stations.'

'Yeah, that does make sense,' Fi said with a shrug. 'It would certainly narrow down where we need to look.'

'I'm still not sure what we do when we find the places,' Guils said. 'We leave someone to watch over each one, what then? What are they going to do if a demon appears?'

'We need an early warning of where they might appear. At least we can do something about it then. We also need to close them once we've figured that out, so we need to find them first.' Fi said.

'Yeah, I suppose.' Guils responded.

'At least with Derek's mates helping us, we have enough people to cover them all, once we find them.' Charlie said, taking a sip of her tea.

'Derek has mates? That's a strange one,' Fi said with a chuckle.

'I have plenty of friends, if you must know,' Derek replied from the door.

'Yeah, sorry, just having a laugh.'

'Well, I've made a list,' Derek said, ignoring Fi's apology. 'I think there are probably another five or six we could check out. Some are in Glasgow, but others are in the borders and Edinburgh.'

'That's not too far away,' Charlie replied, enthusiastically.

'Yes. If we split up, we could probably cover them all in a few days.' Guils added.

'Hang on, I think I might need some help, too,' Lewis said from behind Derek.

'Any luck?' Charlie asked, eagerly.

'Yep,' Lewis said, holding the bundle of swords up in front of a beaming smile.

'Ace!'

'Very nice,' Derek cooed. 'Let's have a look at them.'

'They're not for your collection, Derek,' Lewis said coldly.

'I know that, I just want to take a look. Professional interest, you could say.'

They cleared the table and Lewis unwrapped the swords and laid them out for everyone to see.

'Lovely,' Derek said with a gleam in his eye.

'They're very shiny,' Charlie said.

'Yeah, I think that's the magic, it gives them a glow.' Even in the dull light of the back room the surface of each blade seemed to shimmer and move like a rolling lake of pure gold.

'Can I hold one?' Derek asked, reaching out his hand.

'No!' Lewis barked. 'We don't know what that might do to a human, best be careful.'

'Yes, quite,' Derek responded calmly, but his narrow eyes told the story of his unhappiness at being shouted at by a boy.

'So, how do we find the rest?' Midgy asked.

'A good question, with no answer,' Lewis responded.

71

'That guy Marco's away to do some more digging. He also needed to go and lie down,' Lewis said with a laugh. 'He was ready for bolting, until I explained how much we needed him.'

'Didn't he like you stealing from an old lady?' Charlie asked with a smile.

'Not really, but it was the fact the old lady was a demon that upset him.'

'What!' Charlie said with a start. 'A demon?'

'Yep, the one called Amoyman.'

'What happened?'

'Nothing much,' Lewis said with a shrug. 'I knew it was a demon as soon as we got inside the house, sent it back to hell just like Blaine and The Dark Man.'

'You sent it back on your own?' Guils asked incredulously.

Lewis nodded in reply.

'My God, your power is coming on.'

'It was way easier than the last time. I guess I'm getting the hang of it.'

'How did you twig it was a demon?' Charlie asked.

'It didn't smell right.'

'Really, you can tell?' Charlie asked, raising her eyebrows.

'Yeah, at least I did that time. Pity I couldn't tell with Blaine.'

'How did you know its name?' Charlie asked.

'I asked it. It didn't want to tell me at first, but I can be persuasive.'

'But why ask it, what's that all about?'

'I'm keeping a list. That's three that are back in hell. The Gatherer is at Victoria station, so that's five unaccounted for. I guess most are in hell, but we can't be sure. The quicker we get all the swords and find the portals, the better. How did you get on?'

Charlie updated him on what they found at St Enoch's and their suspicions that a demon had come through a portal there too. She also told him Derek's theory about the stations.

'Seems sound to me. We'll need to wait until Bob returns though, so we can sort out who's going where.'

'Yeah, but what about the remaining swords?' Charlie asked.

'Well, I think there are two with The Gatherer, his own and Blaine's.'

'No way can we get them from The Gatherer.' Fi said.

'I know it'll be hard getting them off him, but we'll have to try; he's a demon after all, and brother to the others. He may even help them.'

'Nah, there's no way he'd help them. He's got a good gig going on there and that would stop if his brothers came through into this world.'

'I suppose, but we're going to have to get them at some point.' Lewis said.

'Let's worry about that later, we've got plenty to be going on with,' Charlie said. 'So we still don't know how we find the four remaining swords?'

'Not until Marco comes back with more info,' Lewis replied, giving Charlie a brief nod of appreciation. They were keen that the crew didn't know that The Dark Man was back yet, so they still officially needed to find four more swords.

'I don't think there's much more we can do until Marco and Bob come back. Best not go looking for the other portals until we've checked in with Bob. Who wants more tea?'

'Got any biscuits?' Lewis asked.

'Yeah, custard creams.' Guils said.

'My favourite.'

'I really don't think we need to wait for Bob you know,' Derek said. 'After all, I know where the abandoned stations are. We can go and look for some and leave the addresses of the others for Bob.'

'Why so keen, Derek? It's been a long day and it's warm in here.'

Derek looked at the blank faces in front of him and sighed. 'I suppose,' he said with a shrug, turning around and going back out to the shop.

'He's high maintenance, that one,' Midgy said quietly.

'You're not wrong,' Charlie replied, laughing.

Derek went out into the main shop and let out a sigh of relief. He wasn't good with people at the best of times, and was finding it particularly hard in the present company. His normal coping mechanism was to be in charge and tell everyone what to do. He was clearly way down the pecking order with this group, however, and being the only one with no magic in a group of magical creatures made it even harder. He didn't like it when he wasn't able to point out where someone was going wrong, or when they said something inaccurate. Even more so when pointing out someone's flaws was likely to get him eaten. He was quite sure Charlie and Lewis wouldn't do that, but he couldn't be sure about the rest. Being chased by a bunch of werewolves wasn't helping to reduce his stress levels either. Just a few short weeks ago he would have laughed if someone had said there were such creatures in the world, but now he was still horrified to learn that there were, and even worse that they were chasing him.

Despite all his misgivings, Derek had to stay close to the lycans. They'd revealed a world to him that he could never have imagined, a world that made his adventures with Abandoned Glasgow look dull by comparison, a world he fully intended to exploit for his own ends, regardless of his stress levels. He let out a sigh and began to scan the display cabinets surrounding him. They were crammed full of objects of all sorts, each one no doubt more expensive than the last. In any other place he'd be tempted to lift an item or two, certain that no one would notice, but not here. The shop reeked of magic, it seemed to ooze out of the walls. Derek thought it was just his imagination at first, what with him only being a human, but the more time he spent in the shop, the more certain he was that the place was alive with magic. It had started the first time he'd entered this place. The objects around him seemed to stare, each one waiting to see if he would pick it up. He was convinced they would start talking to him if he did. He felt the objects watch him now as he moved amongst the shelves and display cabinets. If he listened carefully, he thought he could hear one or two words whisper into the air, 'buy me,' one said, 'take me home,' said another.

Derek shook his head and walked into the centre of the shop. This gave him some distance from the shelves, without having to go into the back room. A round table stood in front of him, covered by a gold-coloured shawl. A gilded cage rested in the centre, with a mechanical parrot clinging to the perch inside.

He leaned in close, marvelling at the craftmanship that it must have taken to make such a piece, wondering at how much it would cost.

'You can't afford me,' the parrot chirped.

Derek shrieked and jumped back from the table.

'You can't afford me Derek. You haven't any money left. You spent it all when you abandoned Cindy.'

Derek felt a shiver run down his spine, his legs wobbled and he staggered backwards until his back hit the end of a shelf. 'What?' was all he could mutter.

The bird looked at him through coal-black eyes, it's beak slowly opening and closing. 'We all know what you did,' it said, in a harsh mechanical voice. 'You let her die so you could live.'

Derek could only stare at the bird in utter terror, his bottom lip trembling wetly.

'You left her all alone in the dark. You're such a naughty boy.'

'I didn't,' Derek was finally able to mumble. 'She was already dead when I left. I couldn't help her, she'd gone.' His hands trembled and his stomach churned as he spoke. A small part of him was convinced that he was going mad, that this was the result of the pressure he'd been under for the last few days. It was this part that helped him speak, otherwise he'd be nothing more than a pool of jelly on the floor.

The bird tilted its head slowly, its beak continuing to open and close. Suddenly the cage door flew open and the bird swooped out and into the air. Derek let out another squeak of terror and sped back into the forest of shelves. He turned blindly left and right, getting away from the mechanical monster his only thought. He bumped into a large stuffed bear and cracked his knee on the corner of an old grandfather clock, the pain bringing him out of his terror fuelled run. He stopped in front of an old painting of a horse drowning in a lake and bent over onto his knees to catch his breath. He rubbed his sore knee and scanned the shelves around him. He didn't remember there being this many before but was glad of the cover. He didn't think the crazy bird would be able to chase him in here. He cocked his head and listened intently for any signs that the creature was near, but all he could hear was the pounding between his ears.

'What the hell am I doing here?' he muttered under his breath. Only silence answered him. He straightened up and tried to get his bearings. He'd turned that many corners that he wasn't sure exactly where he was. 'This place can't be that big,' he thought. He vaguely remembered the size of the shop when he first came in. The cherry coloured front door was framed between two large bay windows that displayed myriad items. The whole place couldn't have been more than thirty feet across in old money. Yet here he was, lost in a small shop, full of shelves and cabinets it simply shouldn't have been big enough to hold. 'Magic,' he said to himself, shaking his head.

'Yes,' a voice whispered around him. 'This place is magic.'

'Who's there? Is that you, Charlie?'

'Magic is magical, don't you agree, my love?'

Derek felt another icy finger run down his spine; it was Cindy's voice. 'I know that's not you.'

'How can you say that to me? I'm the only one who loved you, not even your mother cared for you Derek. She left you to fend for yourself, and that waste of space father of yours let her do it.'

'Shut up!'

'You know it's the truth, my love. I'm the one who cared for you. I care for you still. Even though you left me to die down in that dark hole, I never stopped loving you.'

'Cindy's dead. I don't know what you are, but you're not her.'

'Of course I'm her, you silly boy, and I want you to kiss me. Turn around my love, turn around and kiss me.'

Derek turned around slowly, despite the fear coursing through his body. She was standing in the gloom between two tall shelves, her red eyes staring out at him. Derek whimpered and staggered backwards.

'Don't worry, I just want a kiss. That's all, just a loving kiss. You know you want to kiss me, don't you? You've thought of nothing else since the last time we met.'

Derek shook his head vigorously. 'I don't, I want you to leave me alone.'

'Is that any way to speak to the woman you love?'

'I don't love you, you're not her, she's gone.'

'How can you say that, when I'm standing right in front of you?' The creature slowly emerged from the gloom and glided over to Derek. Her complexion was as pale as a winter's sky. Black lips spread across her face in a knowing smile, revealing sharp white teeth and a deep red tongue. The dimple that Derek had known and loved was still there, as was the tiny mole on her left cheek. It was the eyes that dominated the face, however. They drew Derek in, telling him everything would be alright, if only he gave in to Cindy's wishes. He knew he should run screaming into the backroom to get help, but he was frozen to the spot. He was beyond terror now, his body had become detached from his mind, it refused to obey even the simplest of commands.

'See,' the creature said, placing an icy cold finger onto Derek's cheek, 'I told you everything would be alright if you just gave me that kiss.' She leaned in and brushed her lips against his. His mind screamed for release. This was not his dead girlfriend and the kiss would only do him harm, but his body didn't move. Before he knew it, he was swimming in a sea of the creature's making, floating away into oblivion.

From the gloom of the shelves a black-eyed parrot watched in silence, its beak opening and closing slowly.

MERRY MEETINGS

C alder swam in a sea of pain. His head felt like it was going to split, and shooting pains raced up and down his legs and arms. It hurt every time he took a breath, even his ears ached. He wasn't sure why, but they did. He was spread over a barrel, his arms and legs tied to the floor on either side. It had taken him a few seconds to realise what had happened and where he was when he'd finally come to. The last thing he remembered was driving and staring down the bonnet of an on-coming car. He tried to ease the pressure in his wrists by twisting them slowly, but all that did was send more bolts of pain shooting down his arms.

'I assume that's very painful?' a flat voice asked him from somewhere in the room.

Calder twisted his head around as much as he could, searching for the owner of the voice but all he could see was dark brown walls.

'So, is it?'

'Is it what?' Calder croaked.

'Painful. I took great care in coming up with a suitable punishment for you.'

'Yes, it's painful.'

'Good, but I'm afraid this is only the beginning. When we're done, you'll beg to be put back onto the barrel. Release him.'

Calder groaned in relief as his arms and legs were untied. He was picked up and roughly dragged across the room, before being pushed into a chair. His arms were chained to a ring embedded into the surface of a cold metal table in front of him.

Mr Mono walked into Calder's view and took a seat on the opposite side of the table.

'Oh, hello, long time no see,' Calder said with a cheerfulness he didn't feel. It took all his remaining strength not to try to escape his bonds so he could dive across the table and tear out the creature's heart.

'I suppose you're wondering why you're here?'

'Not really, I betrayed you and your master and now you want your revenge.'

'Well, yes, there is that, but I was referring to being in front of me instead of dead, like your family.'

Calder grimaced at Mono's words and twisted his hands, testing the strength of his bonds.

'I can see that my comments hurt you.'

'The fact that you're breathing hurts me.'

'Good, then we are getting somewhere. After all, hurting you is the point.'

'So, you're keeping me alive so you can torture me? That sounds about right for a demon.'

'Oh, no, we're keeping you alive because we need information. The torture is just a bonus.'

'What information?'

'Swords, portals, that sort of thing.'

'How would I know about any of that?'

Mono nodded and Calder was hit from behind, the shock and pain reverberating down his spine.

'That was just a light tap on the shoulder with a lead pipe. The next time you lie to me I will instruct them to draw blood. Now tell me all you know about swords, and by default I assume all the little princelings know about them too.'

'Where's Scarlett?'

The blow drew blood this time and sent Calder reeling for a minute. When he recovered, he told Mono everything he knew about the swords and what he'd done with Blaine's. He gave up the information easily, if for no other reason than to buy himself time to think. He needed to get out of here and find Lewis's mum.

'So you now know the importance of the swords. It was only a matter of time before that secret was revealed. What about portals? Tell me what you know about them.'

'There are nine, one for each of demon, that's how they come into this world. We don't know how or what the relationship is between the portals and the swords, but we suspect there is one.'

'You have discovered much. A portal is one of the ways my master can enter this world, by far the easiest actually, but it can only be used if you have possession of a sword. They are the key to the portal if you like.'

'So that's how your master was able to come through, you had his sword?'

'Yes, and now you know that, we will have to kill you. I wouldn't want that information getting back to our enemies.'

'You're going to kill me anyway.'

'Yes, but there's no reason why we can't all enjoy ourselves at the same time.'

'Speak for yourself.'

'Tell me Calder, how did you feel when you heard the news? Did your heart break, did you tear your clothes, did you promise revenge?'

'I only felt one thing.'

'What was that?'

'Cold.'

'Interesting. I must admit, I find you humans quite fascinating. Why did you only feel cold?'

'Because that's the best way to serve revenge.'

'What a shame you'll never get a chance, then. If I were you, I'd start getting angry. It will help with what's to come.'

'I know you've already started, Mono. I know you think

80

this is part of the torture, but you're wrong. I don't feel a thing, but it tells me all I need to know about you.'

'Why is that?'

'You need revenge, too, and that's an emotion. So I know you can be hurt and I'm going to hurt you.'

Mono let out a short laugh and shook his head. 'My dear Calder, in just a few short minutes you'll be good for nothing. Give up these silly ideas about revenge. Concentrate on breathing, it's all you'll be able to do, until I stop you.'

'You do a lot of talking for a machine. Come on, Mono, when do we get started?'

Scarlett could smell rotting food. That was the first thing she realised, when she woke up. It was cloying, and it stuck to her nostrils. The next thing she noticed was the pain. It started at the base of her spine and radiated across her back. Then she remembered the car, and the crash, and sat up too quickly. Her head swam and her back groaned. She lay back down and concentrated on not being sick. After a few minutes, she felt well enough to open her eyes. She looked around and, despite the gloom, could make out bars on the far wall. The floor was covered in straw, rotting chunks of fruit and veg were nestled in amongst it, no doubt the cause of the terrible smell. Scarlett made a second attempt at moving and managed to sit up. She waited until another wave of nausea subsided, then tried to stand. Her legs felt like jelly and her back screamed in protest, but she managed to stagger across the cell and fall into the bars. After taking another minute to recover from her exertions, she focussed on her surroundings once again and realised that she was in a cage. Through the bars in front of her she could see a path, with another cage on the opposite side. In front of it was a faded display board proclaiming that the cage held golden snub-nosed monkeys.

'I'm in a zoo,' she muttered, the act of talking sending an electric volt of pain running down the side of her mouth and neck.

'You are my prisoner,' a voice whispered around her.

Scarlett took a step back in shock, got her feet caught beneath her and stumbled over onto her bottom. 'Who's there?' she said after she'd recovered from her fall.

'Tell me, Scarlett, why did you come back?'

'What do you want?'

'I want to know why you came home?'

Scarlett shook her head and refused to answer the voice's question.

'Do you think you can protect him with your silence? I think not. He has taken from me and now I will take everything from him.'

'What are you talking about?'

'He sent me back to my brothers. They were not keen to welcome me home. He made me suffer and I will return the compliment a thousandfold.'

'He's just a boy.'

'He is a prince of the blood, and my enemy. You are my enemy too; such a shame, we could have made a strong alliance.'

'I'd never team up with you.'

'Why not? You've teamed up with my kind before. A very fruitful union, so I've heard.'

Scarlett knew who was speaking, and the thought of him being so close sent shivers down her spine. She'd heard he'd been sent back to hell, but here he was, as large as life. He was after something from her, that much was obvious. If he wasn't, she was sure she'd be dead by now.

'What you want?'

'For you to suffer of course. He needs to know the full extent of my fury and he will when I sate my anger on your soul.'

Scarlett swallowed hard. She was used to pain, but this was The Dark Man, and he could invent new ways for her to suffer.

Showing a bravery she didn't feel, she stumbled to her feet and walked towards the bars. 'You're such a coward, you can't even show yourself to me. Come on, try your best, I'll rip you limb from limb.'

'We'll see,' a voice said from behind her. Scarlett wheeled around to face red eyes the colour of hot coals, and a mouth contorted in a wicked grin. Her battle cry turned to a scream before it had finished leaving her mouth.

Meanwhile, Back at the Shop

B ob sat down with a sigh and kicked off his boots. 'Got any of that tea left?'

Charlie poured him a steaming cup and he took a gulp with a satisfied grunt, then leaned back in his chair, his back making little popping sounds as he stretched.

'What did you find?' Charlie asked, impatient to hear his news.

'A dead body laid out on a table, that's what. It'd been killed in some sort of ritual by the looks of it. That and loads of black oily smudges on the floor. No idea what they were.'

'Nothing else?'

'Nope. I figured a dead body was enough.'

'Yeah, of course,' Charlie replied, shaking inside at how easy it was for her now to speak about dead bodies and killing.

'There was something else, though. I saw a symbol on the outside of the station. High up and hard to see, but it smelt of magic too, that's how I saw it.'

'What was it?'

'Not sure, but I think it's a way that their followers might know there's a portal on site.'

'That makes sense,' Lewis said as he entered the room. 'If these places are supposed to be secret, there has to be a way for their followers to find where they are in each station. The railway signs won't tell them that.'

'I still can't fathom why anyone would want to follow a demon,' Charlie said.

'You mean, like we all did with Blaine?' Lewis asked.

'Well, yeah, but we didn't know.'

'I suspect some of their followers don't know, either. Not the whole story. The line between good and evil is a thin one. What's that saying about the road to hell is paved with good intentions?' Bob said.

'It's paved with abandoned train stations for us,' Charlie replied with a laugh.

'At least we know we can identify the stations that have portals, then, if they have that symbol. The railway sign tells us the station and the symbol tells us where,' Lewis suggested.

'Yeah, that sounds about right and should save us having to search for too long. So, what have you two been up to?' Bob asked.

Lewis and Charlie filled Bob in on what had been happening while he was gone, and Lewis showed him the swords they'd retrieved.

'They're amazing. Terrifying, but amazing. It's like they speak to you. I don't like what they say.'

'Me neither, but we need them if we're going to beat that lot.'

'We need to keep them safe. If they suspect we have them, they'll come at us all guns blazing.'

'They'll come after us anyway,' Charlie said with a laugh.

'Has anyone seen Calder?' Bob asked suddenly.

'Nope not seen him for ages.'

'That's strange. He was doing me a favour, but he should be back by now. I'd best give him a call.'

'What's he been up to?'

'Never mind, it's a secret.'

'We seem to have a lot of them,' Charlie said quietly, 'I'd have thought you'd learnt your lesson with Blaine?'

'Yeah, but this is a good one, trust me.'

'Trust; that seems like a very important word to me,' Derek said from the doorway.

'Oh, hello Derek,' Bob said, without enthusiasm.

Derek entered the room and gracefully sat down at their small table. He had a quiet smile on his face, and eyes that darted around like they were looking for traps.

'Are you OK?' Charlie asked.

'Yes, a very important word indeed,' Derek said, ignoring her. 'Take our blood royals here. They trust you Bob, but you don't seem to trust them in return.'

'What the hell are you talking about?'

'You have your little secrets that you keep them in the dark. You've been doing that since they were children, I think.'

'I've kept them safe, we all have. You don't know anything, Derek.'

'I know enough to question your motives.'

'What are you going on about?' Lewis asked impatiently.

'I think Bob suspected Blaine for a very long time, but he didn't tell you. In fact, I know he deliberately put you in danger. Now, when you've finally come into your power, he still keeps secrets from you. Tell us all what Calder's been up to, Bob.'

'Like I said, it's a surprise,' Bob replied, looking hard at Derek.

'There you have it. Secrets and a clear lack of trust.'

'I think Bob's proven himself time and again Derek, not that you'd know anything about that. You, on the other hand, have yet to show us you can be trusted.'

'Really? After I brought you the information about the portals and took you to one of them. Did I not prove myself in the sewers? How much more must I do?'

'All you've proven so far is that you're in this for yourself,' Bob said.

'Aren't we all? At least I'm honest about my intentions. Can you say the same, Bob?'

'Yes, I can. Now shut up.'

Derek smiled and lowered his head. He had achieved his goal. He could see the tiny seeds of doubt already planted behind Charlie's eyes.

'So we need to go to the other stations, and Lewis needs to wait on this Marco fella?' Bob asked, quickly changing the subject.

'Yep. I can't really do much more until he shows.'

'There's something else,' Charlie said. 'You found a dead body at Creagan, and we found one at St Enoch's and that can only mean one thing; the demons are coming through into this world.'

'How can you be so sure?' Bob asked.

'I can't be, but it's a bit of a coincidence, don't you think? We find dead bodies at two abandoned stations that we think contain portals into hell?'

Bob pursued his lips and nodded. 'Yep, it makes sense if you look at it like that.'

'But as long as we have the swords, they can't come through, right?' Lewis asked.

'They could have used swords we haven't found yet, or they're already through and we just got lucky finding the swords, after the fact,' Charlie mused. 'Either way, we have to continue looking for the portals and the swords. We've made a good start. We know of two portals, maybe a third, and we have three swords.'

'And we know where a fourth and a fifth are,' Lewis added.

'Yeah we just need to find the rest, get the two off The Gatherer, and then work out how to destroy them, simple.' Charlie said.

'Let's not forget we need to visit all those other stations to find the remaining portals.' Lewis reminded them.

'Something we need to get started on as soon as, and thanks to Derek, we have a good idea where they are,' Bob said with a nod in Derek's direction.

'I don't know about you, but I need to sleep first,' Charlie said.

'Yes, a good night's sleep might be good for everyone,' Derek suggested.

Lewis's phone began to ring. He pressed the answer button and listened intently. 'Are you sure?' he asked, then grunted at the reply, before putting down his phone.

'Doesn't look like I'm getting any sleep after all. That was Marco, he's got a lead on the other swords, but we need to go now. Where's Guils and Fi?'

'They've gone home.'

'I could come with you?' Charlie suggested.

'No, you look done in; best get some sleep.'

'Midgy's here somewhere; he could help.'

Lewis shook his head. He didn't want the untested lycan crashing about if things got serious.

'I could help,' Derek offered eagerly.

'No, we need you to help find the other stations,' Lewis replied quickly. Looking after Derek the man-child was an even worse idea than taking Midgy along. 'OK, I'm outta here,' he said, draining his cup and standing up.

'Where are you going? It might be best if we know where you are just in case you get into trouble,' Derek asked.

'It's OK, I know how to get myself out of trouble,' Lewis replied. He paused and looked at Derek's eager face. There was something different about him, but he couldn't quite put his finger on it. 'OK, troops, see you later.'

The room settled into quiet after Lewis left, each person lost in their own thoughts.

'I hope he's OK,' Derek said quietly.

'He'll be fine; it's whoever he bumps into that has to watch out,' Bob replied.

'Yes, there is that.'

'I better give Calder a ring, he should have returned by now,' he said, standing up and leaving the room.

EVEN MORE MERRY MEETINGS

Jillian shivered and pulled her coat tighter around her shoulders. She hated the cold and damp, it seemed to seep into her bones and stay there. Her fingers ached, and she cursed the fact that she'd forgotten her gloves. She was sure that it was colder than it was supposed to be in this place, the ghosts of the dead no doubt helping to lower the temperature. Her breath came out in long white clouds as she made her way through the abandoned zoo, the empty cages staring mournfully out at her as she passed, the contents long since escaped or dead. She heard a low growl come from somewhere in front of her and stopped with a sigh.

'I'm here to see your master, I mean no harm.'

'So you say,' a figure said as it appeared from the shadows in front of her.

'If I meant harm, you would know,' Jillian responded menacingly.

'This is his seat, you cannot harm him here.'

'So you say, now take me to him.'

'What's your business?'

'That's between him and me; are you going to take me to him, or do I have to find him myself?'

The figure smiled and nodded his head. 'Very well, I will take you to him.'

The guide took Jillian along myriad paths, winding past empty cages and a broken play park, around a dilapidated shop and through an ancient seal house. Eventually she was led into what looked like a monkey enclosure, complete with tyre swing and tree house.

'Wait here,' he said, before turning around and leaving.

'Aren't you going to offer me a coffee while I wait?' Jillian called after him. She was met with silence as a response. 'I guess not.' She pulled her coat closer around her once again. It was definitely ice cold in the monkey enclosure.

'We meet again, angel,' a voice whispered from the dark recesses of the crumbling monkey house.

'Hello demon.'

'Why have you come here this time?'

'To deliver a message, nothing more.'

'From your master I presume?'

'Who else?'

'Go on then, deliver your message.'

'It stops now.'

'Is that it?'

'Yes.'

'That's a very short message. What stops now, I wonder?

'You know what. The war, the fighting, your meddling on this plane.'

'Ah, I see. Well, I'm afraid that is not in my gift, as I'm sure your master knows,' The Dark Man said.

'It can be, if you stop first.'

'And let my brothers or the lycans kill me, or worse, send me back to hell? I think not.'

'It can't go on like this. You risk exposing our world to the humans, and my master cannot allow that.'

'Your master is all powerful, and can stop this anytime she chooses.'

'You know that's not how it works.'

'Oh, yes, free will, what a lovely concept.'

'That you and your brothers chose to exploit to spread fear and greed.'

'We never said we were perfect.'

'I take it your answer is no, then?'

'I cannot give you what is not in my gift, she knows that, and sets a trap for me. It's very obvious, rain down on us, I say. Send us all back to hell, but do not ask me to stop. That I can never do.'

Jillian nodded. She knew this would be his response, but she had to try. It was hard being on the side of good, and giving evil a choice, especially when there really wasn't one if you were a demon.

'Will you take this order to the other side?'

'Yes, and any of your brothers who are on this side of the plane.'

'You will get the same response from them.'

'Perhaps, but I have to try.'

'Yes, she does like to be seen to do the right thing, doesn't she? Before she goes and gives a child cancer, or kills a village in a flood. And you call me a demon.'

'Do not try to understand her will.'

'Oh, I would never dream of it, angel. Is that all you have to say?'

'For now.'

'I wish you a pleasant evening, then. Oh, and say hello to our blood royals when you see them.'

'I'm sure they will all be thrilled that you're back.'

'I can't wait to meet them again.'

'No doubt.' Jillian shook her head and turned to leave.

'Can you pass on a message to my lycan friends?'

Jillian turned back, intrigued. 'What message?'

'Tell Bob that I look forward to a happy reunion.'

'Is that it?'

'Yes, he'll know what I mean.'

Jillian closed her eyes and sighed. It was going to be a long night.

The shop was cloaked in darkness when she arrived, its large bay windows covered in a shroud of black. Jillian gritted her teeth and tapped her foot irritably. She'd expected it to be a hive of activity now that The Dark Man had returned and was eager to get this done so she could get out of the cold and get on with her real work. Being a glorified messenger was beneath her.

'Bloody lycans,' she cursed under her breath.

'Oh, come on now, we're not all that bad,' a voice said from behind her.

Startled, Jillian swung around to face the voice, and was met with Bob's smiling face.

'You must be Bob,' she said with a sigh.

'I am, who are you?'

'My name is Jillian Lightfoot, I am a messenger from the one.'

'The one what?'

'*The* one.'

'Oh, you mean *her*? I guess that makes you an angel, then?'

'Yes. You don't seem very surprised to be meeting a celestial being.'

'If you've seen one angel, you've seen them all,' Bob said with a shrug, 'Anyway, I'm busy, we have a crisis to deal with, so please tell me why you're here, skulking around outside the shop?'

'I'm not skulking. I thought it would still be open, and from what I've heard, you always have a crisis to deal with.'

'Far less now that Blaine's gone, things are different. I assume you know all about Blaine, you being from above and watching over us all?'

'Yes. Where're Lewis and Charlie?'

'I'm not surprised you know about them too. Charlie's sleeping, Lewis is away, do you want to speak to her?'

'No, you'll do. I have a message.'

'From her?'

'Yes, of course from her. It's a simple one; stop, now.'

'Stop what?'

'Fighting demons and werewolves.'

'Oh, sure, yeah, we'll stop right away,' Bob said with a chuckle.

'This is serious, the humans are starting to notice, and she can't allow that.'

'Well, then, she can stop the demons. You know they'll never stop, and we have to defend ourselves, and this world, and the humans too come to think of it.'

'Yeah, he said something similar.'

'Who?'

'The Dark Man.'

'You've seen him? Where is he?' Bob asked.

'You know I can't tell you that.'

'Of course not. The kids will be disappointed that you refused to help us, they've only just sent him back to hell.'

'Well, he managed to come back quickly, once they got rid of Blaine. He was helping to keep his brothers on the other side.'

'We didn't know that. It took a lot to send them both back to hell.'

'Which is why she wants you all to stop. It will not end well, for either side.'

'She's all powerful, why can't she stop them?'

'Because of free will, of course. Don't you think she would have intervened otherwise?'

'So what will she do if we don't stop?'

'I don't know, but it won't be good. She would have to treat both sides equally'

'Sorry, but we'll need to take that chance.'

'Come on, Bob, I'm on your side, remember. You're the good guys.'

'It's nice to know, but I'm sorry; there's no way we can leave ourselves open like that. We have to finish them.'

Jillian nodded. She had expected to hear that from both sides, but was still disappointed all the same. 'OK, but remember I tried.'

'Why doesn't she help us? Like you said, we're the good guys. Never mind all that free will stuff.'

'Even she can't ignore free will. If she did, it would unleash a war in heaven, and we don't want another one of those,' Jillian said, shuddering at the memory of the violence and bloodshed the last war caused.

'You lot certainly do work in mysterious ways.'

'You have no idea.'

'So, what do I tell them?'

'Tell them God wants them to stop and will look at ways to stop both sides if you don't.'

'Even though she can't intervene on either side. It sounds very convenient to me.'

'Just tell them.'

'OK, but their answer will be the same as mine, you know that?'

'Unfortunately, I do.'

KELVINGROVE

Lewis wasn't sure what surprised him the most, the fact that they had got into the basement of the world renowned Kelvingrove Art Gallery and Museum so easily, or that Marco was comfortable with a little bit of breaking and entering. He didn't strike Lewis as the type who would be happy breaking the law, but it had been his idea to crowbar open one of the small basement windows to gain entry into the museum.

'My dad used to work here, and he says none of the basement windows are alarmed. They figure there's nothing in there anyone would want to steal, seeing as all the good stuff is up in the main museum. You don't want to go anywhere near that lot up there, it's alarmed up the wazoo.' Lewis had no idea what a wazoo was, but it didn't sound good.

They'd first gained entry into a large room that looked like some sort of lab. There were microscopes and all sorts of other scientific equipment on the tables that Lewis didn't recognise. A multitude of antiques and ancient artefacts also littered the benches.

'This is where they check out the authenticity of the

artefacts, and do conservation work,' Marco whispered.

'Cool, where are the swords kept?'

'In a room down the hall. They're not locked up or anything, according to my dad.'

'As long as we can get them and get out of here quick, I don't mind if they've got an armed guard.'

They exited the room and came into a long corridor with doors inset on either side. Names like Store 1, and Testing Room 3 were displayed on them as they passed. One was called Invasion Room 2. Lewis didn't know why you needed one room with a name like that, never mind two of them.

'Here it is,' Marco whispered as they reached the end of the corridor. This room didn't have a name displayed on the door, it simply said 'Private'. Despite Marco's reassurances Lewis fully expected the room to be locked but the handle turned with a small squeak and the door opened inward to reveal a dark chasm beyond.

Marco turned on his flashlight and panned it across the room. The light revealed long lines of deep metal shelves, each one containing myriad artefacts.

'Which shelf are they on?' Lewis asked in a whisper.

'No idea, my dad just said they were kept in this room.'

'OK, you go left, I'll go right, and we'll make our way down the shelves and into the middle. Anything that looks sword shaped could be them. Have you got another flashlight?'

'No, I thought you wouldn't need one.'

'Why?'

'Well, you're a werewolf, I figured you could see in the dark.'

'Seriously?' Lewis asked with a sigh. 'It doesn't work like that, and I'm a lycan, not a werewolf; don't confuse the two.'

'Look, I'll put it on top of this shelf, that way we'll both be able to see what we're doing,' Marco said, reaching out and putting the flashlight high up on one of the shelves.'

'It'll have to do, we can't put the room lights on in case someone sees. OK, let's get going.'

They began making their way down the shelves, pausing every now and again to unwrap packages. The room was full of artefacts of every sort, from masks and spears, to china bowls, cups, vases and the odd marble head. There was even an ancient looking sewing machine, and what might once have been a typewriter. Lewis grew concerned that they wouldn't find what they were looking for, as they neared the centre of the room, until Marco let out a soft shout of triumph.

'Found them' he whispered as loud as he dare.

Lewis rushed around the shelves to find Marco holding one of the swords up in front of his face, the gold gleaming off his eyes, despite the gloom. 'They really are amazing,' he cooed.

Like the others they'd rescued from the demon, the surface of the sword seemed to ripple and move, like the weapon was alive.

'They're pure evil, that's what they are,' Lewis said, gently taking the sword out of Marco's hands.

'Yeah, I can see that,' Marco said, reluctantly letting go.

The sword fitted easily into Lewis's palm, like it was meant to be there. He felt a soft thrill go up his arm as he took in the sword's weight. Swallowing hard, he peered closely at the sword's hilt and spied the tell-tale signs he'd seen on the other swords. He picked up the second sword and hefted them both in front of him. For a moment, he could see himself charging into battle, cutting down werewolves and demons left and right, using the power of the swords to vanquish his enemies.

'Are you OK?' Marco asked. His voice seeming to come from a million miles away.

'I'll kill them all.'

'What? Lewis, are you OK?' Marco asked, more insistently.

Lewis tore his mind away from the vision in front of him. It took all his strength to come away from the blood and horror that wielding the swords was showing him. With a supreme effort, he put them both back onto the shelf, instantly feeling better once contact with the swords was broken. 'That was strange.'

'Yeah, you seemed to disappear for a moment there. What happened?'

'No idea. Something happened as soon as I picked up both swords.'

'Then don't do that again. Come on, we better get out of here, the place may not be alarmed but they definitely have security guards.'

A deep growl reverberated off the shelves, making the pots stored there rattle and shake. The hairs stood up on the back of Lewis's neck, and he had to stop himself from automatically changing.

'What the hell was that?' Marco asked.

'I don't know, but it's not a werewolf.'

'How do you know?'

'Just a feeling.'

'The sound came from the corridor.'

Lewis nodded in reply and made his way slowly to the door. 'Look after the swords,' he said over his shoulder. He was hit with the strong smell of rotting meat as soon as he emerged out of the room. It seemed to wrap around his face and tighten his throat.

Another growl came from the other end of the corridor. It rattled the doors on either side and vibrated along the floor, and up into Lewis's feet. Whatever was making the sound was huge, and it was coming his way.

Lewis turned and was immediately hit with the gagging stench of rotting meat, now that his sense of smell was a hundred times greater. He crouched on the floor and whimpered as his eyes streamed. The hairs stood out on his back, and an overwhelming urge to run hit him. It was a feeling he'd never had before, and it made him shake to his bones. With an enormous effort he raised himself off the floor and made his way down the corridor. The stench increased the further he went, and he involuntarily held his breath, to avoid it.

Turning a corner, he was met with a sight straight out of

hell. A large beast stood in front of him. It had the head of a bull, topped with sharp horns, and the muscular body of a man, standing upright on two hoofed feet. Eyes the colour of blood turned to look at Lewis as he emerged from the corridor. They contemplated him for a moment, then the beast let out a roar and charged. Unsure what to do, instinct took over, as he changed and prepared for impact.

The monster hit him square on the chest, sending him flying backwards and through a nearby wall. Lewis smashed into a row of shelves, sending the contents flying all around him. He eventually came to rest in a heap, covered in broken bits of pottery and glass. The beast appeared in the Lewis shaped hole in the wall and let out another roar.

Incensed at being so easily flung aside, Lewis jumped up and let out a roar of this own, before leaping forward and smashing into the beast. The momentum took them both out into the corridor and up against a door on the opposite side. Lewis snarled and snapped at the monster, trying to rip open its throat, but the creature pushed back at him and managed to avoid his snapping jaws. It grabbed Lewis by the throat and launched him down the corridor.

Lewis scrambled to his feet as quickly as he could, and charged at the creature again, this time dropping low before impact, and taking its legs from under it. He jumped on top before the beast could right itself and began pounding on its head and torso. The creature writhed underneath him and managed to get a hold of one of Lewis's arms. It squeezed hard, then flung him back down the corridor. This was without a doubt the most powerful beast he had encountered so far, and small seeds of doubt began to grow inside him as he stood up once again. The beast stood up too and waited for Lewis to charge. Shaking himself down, Lewis did the only thing he could. He let out another roar and charged. Halfway down the corridor he changed back into a human and dropped onto the ground as he approached the creature, the momentum taking him between its legs. He jumped up once he was clear and raced towards the room where Marco was waiting with the swords. The creature turned around, momentarily confused at its prey's disappearance, then let out a roar of frustration as it saw him running away.

'Let's go!' Lewis screamed as he reached the doorway. Marco didn't need telling a second time, he'd heard the altercation in the corridor. He rushed out of the room, with his arms full of swords.

'What's going on?' he gasped.

'No time, let's go!

They ran down the corridor with the beast in hot pursuit. Turning yet another corner they emerged into a large foyer with glass shelves on either side, displaying an array of ancient artefacts. Lewis turned and prepared to face the creature once again.

'Keep going Marco, there's a door on the opposite side.'

'Maybe we can kill it with these?' Marco said, brandishing the swords in front of him.

'I don't think so, keep running.'

The creature walked slowly into the foyer, scanning the room for signs of danger, then stopped and stared at Lewis.

'Who sent you?' Lewis asked.

The creature simply stared back at him, breathing heavily through its nose and filling the room with its pungent aroma.

'Who sent you?' Marco asked, walking forward and raising one of the swords in front of him.

'No!' Lewis screamed, but it was too late. The creature lunged forward and with lightning speed removed Marco's head from his shoulders with one swipe of its massive hand. Lewis's scream quickly turned into a roar as he changed back into a lycan. Enraged, he launched himself at the monster, smashing into it and sending them both reeling backwards, into one of the glass cabinets.

He punched and kicked and snapped at the monster, all sense of self lost, as he boiled over with rage and loathing. Cuts began to appear on the creature's face and body, black blood seeping onto the floor. Its roars turned to screams of pain as Lewis continued his attack. With a monumental effort, the monster managed to get its legs underneath Lewis's body and propel him backwards. He scraped along the floor and came to rest on the opposite side of the foyer, turning back into a human so he could use his hands to stop his momentum. The creature was upon him before he could recover and began to beat him about the head and body with its powerful fists. Lewis saw stars as one blow sent his head back into the floor. He was sure he was going to die underneath the blows, and reached out his hands in a desperate attempt to find anything that would help. A shard of glass or a broken bit of pottery would be enough, but his hand curled around the hilt of one of the swords. He raised it up off the floor and smashed the hilt into the side of the creature's head.

It fell backwards and lay in a heap on the floor, blood slowly seeping onto the ground around the new head wound.

Lewis staggered to his feet, panting for breath and desperately trying to regain his composure. The creature was the most powerful being he'd encountered to date, far more powerful than the demons he'd sent back to hell. When he felt more in control of himself, he walked drunkenly towards Marco's body. It lay at an awkward angle, one arm reaching out for the sword that was no longer in his hand. The side of his head had been caved in by the force of the monster's attack, his one remaining eye staring out into nothing.

'I'm sorry,' Lewis managed to croak, 'you didn't know what you were getting into.' He closed the eye then went to pick up the swords.

He could hear sounds coming some way off down the corridor and realised the museum's guards must be on their way to investigate the noise. The creature began to stir as he picked up the first sword, it moaned and let out a series of weak growls.

'Time to go,' Lewis said to himself, looking around for the room where they'd come in. It was at this moment that he realised he had no idea where the room was. Not wishing to stay around and explain why there was a dead body and a mythical creature lying on the floor, he raced towards the first door and opened it. Unfortunately, it led into a cleaners' cupboard. Panicking as the sound of approaching footsteps grew louder, he raced across the foyer and opened a door on the opposite side. This led into a large lab with a row of windows on the far wall. He closed the door behind him with a sigh of relief and made his way over to the windows. Each one was firmly locked. By now he could hear the sound of shocked voices coming from outside the room. Then a growl and a scream. Lewis was about to rush out to save the guards when he heard footsteps racing away, quickly followed by a growling, snarling sound that could only be the monster. He opened the door enough to see the foyer beyond. It was empty, apart from the Marco's prone body. Not knowing what else to do, he shut the door and raced back to the windows. Not caring how much noise he made, he smashed the nearest one to him and climbed out. The air was cold and fresh after the rotting stench percolating around the basement. It was quiet outside, a stark contrast to the noise and horror he'd just encountered. Pausing, he turned back to look into the basement. A part of him felt like he should go back and retrieve Marco's body. But a greater part of him was saying he should run away, as fast as he could. That part won the argument. Lewis rose up and raced away from the museum as fast as his legs could carry him.

THE GREAT ESCAPE

S carlett rolled over onto her back and groaned. Her arms and legs ached, and her head felt like it was going to split. They'd been gentle on her, so they said, but it felt like she'd been hit by a truck. At least she was in better shape than Calder. He lay in a heap in the far corner of the cage. He hadn't moved since they'd brought him in and dumped him there. Scarlett wanted to roll over and see if he was OK, but her body refused to move. It had taken all her strength just to roll over onto her back.

'Calder,' she managed to croak. Her mouth felt like sandpaper, and she would have given her right arm for a glass of water at that moment. 'Calder, are you OK?'

Calder didn't move.

'Speak to me.'

'He can't, they've broken him,' a voice said from beyond the cage.

Scarlett jerked her head around and immediately regretted it, as jolts of pain stabbed into her. A man stood in front of her, his arms casually resting through the bars. 'What do you want werewolf?'

'That's no way to greet a friend.'

'You're no friend to me.'

'I'll not bother rescuing you then.'

'What are you talking about?'

'I assume you and your friend want to get out of here?'

'He sent you, didn't he? He sent you to torment me with freedom. I'm not falling for it.'

'No, he didn't, Bob sent me.' The man opened his hand to reveal a heart-shaped charm, with half the heart missing. Scarlett gasped at the sight; she owned the other half. They'd agreed long ago that they would use the charms as a secret sign. It said she should trust this man.

'Can you sit up?'

Scarlett stared at him before replying. This could still be a trap to torment her even further, but there was no way The Dark Man could know about the charm or get the other half from Bob.

'I think so, but I don't know about Calder.'

'Let me worry about him. I can carry him as long as you can walk.'

'I can walk,' she said, groaning as she tried to sit up. Her head swam as she lifted herself into a sitting position and she gasped for breath as she held herself there, trembling.

'Are you sure?' the man asked dubiously.

'I'm sure, just worry about him.'

The man produced a key and opened the cage. 'We need to be quick, I don't know how long we've got before they discover you're gone.'

Scarlett managed to drag herself upwards and stood leaning against the bars as her saviour – well, she hoped he was her saviour – gently lifted Calder off the floor and carried him out of the cage. She followed them out, half expecting to see The Dark Man standing further down the path, laughing at them, but the area was cold and covered in a light dusting of snow.

The man slowly followed a winding path past myriad empty cages. Scarlett managed to keep up at the start, but tired quickly and stopped often to catch her breath. Her whole body ached, and each little movement sent jolts of pain running down her arms and legs, but she needed to put that out of her mind if she was ever going to get out of this place alive. After what seemed an eternity, they came to a large fence that marked the boundary of the zoo. The man gently put Calder onto the ground and turned to Scarlett.

'This is as far as I go. There's a gap in the fence and a friend is waiting on the other side.'

'Why don't you come with us?' Scarlett asked, through long gasps of breath.

'I need to stay. I can do more good here.'

'Oh, I think you've done enough good for now,' a soft voice said from further back down the path. The man hissed and leaped into a defensive position in front of Scarlett.

'Thank you, Scarlett, I knew your incarceration would prove useful and I was right. We had fun and finally found our spy. I knew Bob and his cronies wouldn't be able to resist a rescue. Congratulations, you've been a great help.'

'Scarlett, take Calder and get through the fence, I'll hold them off,' the man said over his shoulder.

'Yes, take Calder if you can, we've no more use for him anyway. Mr Mono has had his fun,' The Dark Man said cheerily.

Scarlett hobbled over to Calder and tried to pick him up. It was no use, she didn't have the strength. 'I can't,' she gasped.

'Oh, dear, have we tired you out?'

Scarlett fell to her knees and leaned into the silent man. 'Calder, you need to get up, we can get out of here, but only if you get up.'

There was no movement at first, then he opened his eyes and stared at her.

'Get up,' she hissed. 'Get up for your family. You'll never get justice if you lay here.'

He stared at her, then slowly raised himself onto his elbows.

'Well done,' The Dark Man said, clapping. 'Now kill him, my children,' he said to the werewolves waiting behind him. They rushed forward in a wave of sound, all teeth and claws.

Scarlett closed her eyes and waited for the inevitable. She didn't want to watch them race towards her and there was no way one rogue werewolf was going to defeat The Dark Man's minions and save her and Calder. She felt a rush of breeze and felt one thing then another and another brush past her. Opening her eyes, she watched as a stream of lycans crashed towards the lone werewolf's defence. The battle was intense, violent and quick. Dead or dying werewolves lay on the ground, as blood slowly seeped into the dark earth. Lycans in different stages of transformation stood in front of her, but she couldn't see her saviour.

'Come on we need to get out of here,' a woman said, holding out her hand. 'Never mind The Dark Man, you lot, he's run away, the coward, we need to get out of here,' she shouted at her companions.

'Where is he?' Scarlett croaked.

'If you mean Stan, he's dead. Come on, we need to go.'

'Was that his name?'

'Yes, he was one of Bob's oldest friends. He'll be devastated.'

'I've never heard of him,' Scarlett mumbled as she was helped up off the floor.

'That's the idea. It wouldn't have done for anyone to know about him, even we didn't know he was here. He called Bob to tell him you'd been taken and were at the old zoo. Can you walk?'

'Yes,' Scarlett gasped as she stood on her own two feet, 'but take it slow.'

They led her through the gap in the fence and out onto the road. She half expected a wave of werewolves to come out and attack them, but it was eerily quiet. She was led to a waiting car and sighed as she sat down in the passenger seat. The car pulled away and disappeared into the night. Scarlett let out another sigh, but this one was of relief. She never expected to survive the zoo, and a pang of guilt hit her stomach as she thought about Stan, a person she didn't know, who'd risked his life to save her and Calder.

'Where's Calder?'

'In the other car.'

'Are we safe? Will the werewolves chase after us and try to attack? They must be angry that we attacked them and their master in his lair?'

'They didn't the last time we attacked the zoo, but who knows, we'll deal with them if they do.'

'What's your name?'

'Guils.'

'Thank you, Guils, you saved my life.'

'Don't mention it, anything for the prince's mum. I just can't believe that monster is back, we only just got rid of him,' Guils replied, shaking her head. 'I thought Bob was lying when he told me.'

'Yeah, he's back,' Scarlett replied, then she smiled at what Guils had called her son. She'd forgotten that her baby boy was now a prince, and his best friend a princess. She bit her bottom lip at the thought of meeting him again. What would he be like now that he'd come into his power? Would he forgive her for abandoning him? Could he ever trust her again? She'd kept so much from him, with good reason. It was to protect him. But she wasn't sure he'd see it that way. Especially after all he'd been through recently, all of which he'd had to endure without her help.

Scarlett loved her son unconditionally. There was nothing she wouldn't do for him. But she knew he'd be angry because he thought she'd left him to fend for himself when he needed her the most. She would forever feel guilty that she'd left him to go and search for a demon in Edinburgh, and that Bob had convinced her that he would keep Lewis safe until she returned. That reasoning seemed silly now, especially after Bob told her about the power Lewis had; he could clearly look after himself. The idea of him being a powerful prince of the blood frightened and enthralled her at the same time. She felt a pang of guilt that she hadn't been there the first time he'd changed, and that she hadn't been able to support him afterwards.

'Where are we going?'

'To the shop, Bob will be waiting.'

'Where's my son?'

'Out on a job.'

'Will there be tea?'

'Always,' Guils replied with a laugh.

Scarlett settled back into her seat and for the first time since she'd come back to Glasgow, was able to close her eyes and relax a little. Before she knew it, she was being shaken awake.

'We're here.'

'Oh, OK,' she replied, wiping drool from the side of her mouth.

It was early morning by the time they arrived at the shop and the place was a hive of activity once again, its golden light spilled out onto the pavement where the car was parked, the large bay windows displaying an inviting scene, as a large gathering of people appeared to laugh and joke with each other. It seemed a million miles away from the shop she had last visited, when Blaine owned it.

'It looks like there's a party going on.'

'Not really, it just feels like that ever since we got rid of Blaine.'

'I guess that's certainly something to celebrate for a long time.'

'Yeah I guess so,' Guils replied, laughing. 'By the way, most don't know about The Dark Man's return just yet, we'll tell them after tea, I'd appreciate if you don't say anything just yet. I'm only just getting used to the idea myself.'

Scarlett nodded in reply, although she was certain they'd all know long before their tea went cold.

They entered the shop and were quickly enveloped by a warmth that was shrouded in the smell of tea. Scarlett smiled; she'd come home.

There was a chorus of welcomes as they moved into the room, followed by hugs and back slapping. They all welcomed her back like a long lost hero. She knew some of them but had always made it a point of steering clear of Blaine's troops as much as she could. Another attempt to protect Lewis that had clearly been a mistake. There was a comradery amongst the lycans that Lewis could clearly benefit from.

'You took your time,' a voice said to her from the back of the shop. Bob was leaning against the door frame with a big smile on his face. He beckoned her into the back shop and disappeared behind the curtain. She followed him into the small room, giving him a fierce hug before sitting down on a pile of books.

'I'm sorry.'

'What for?'

'We should have known they'd come after you when you returned. I thought we'd managed to keep it quiet. Clearly not.'

'The Dark Man has spies everywhere.'

'Even here, it would seem.'

'Then we have to be careful.'

'I thought we *were* being careful.'

'Your man's dead, I'm sorry.'

'Yeah, they phoned and told me. He was a good friend, I'll miss him. He was the one who told me you'd been taken.' Bob replied, with a tear in his eye. 'That monster has only just returned, I didn't think he'd have knowledge of the guy I'd manged to plant in his troops before Lewis sent him back to hell.'

'Where is he?' Scarlett asked after a minute's silence.

'Out, but he's expected back soon.'

'And Charlie?'

'She popped out for something to eat with Derek.'

'Derek?'

'I'll tell you about him later.'

'How is he, Bob?'

'He's doing great. You'll see for yourself. His power is amazing.'

Bob felt nervous now that Scarlett was back. He'd convinced Lewis not to go looking for her after they'd sent Blaine back to hell, even though Lewis was keen to do so. He'd lied and told him that she'd left because The Dark Man was after her power and that she suspected Blaine was up to no good too. He wasn't about to tell him the real reason she'd left in such a hurry. His explanation made less sense the longer she stayed away after Blaine and The Dark Man had gone. Now, weeks later, Lewis was convinced she'd abandoned him and fell into a foul mood anytime Bob mentioned her name.

'Is that all you're bothered about, his power?'

'No of course not, but you know it's the only way he can protect himself. He sent two demons back to hell.'

'Yeah, I heard. It didn't last long though, did it?'

'No, but if he did it once, then …' Bob left the rest unsaid.

'I know, but it's dangerous,' Scarlett said, fiercely.

'This was never going to be easy, we all know that. We're in a war, Scarlett. One not of our making. The only way to survive is to fight. Anyway, how are you?'

'I've been better.'

'Did you manage to find him in Edinburgh?'

She shook her head in response.

'What did they do to you?'

Scarlett shook her head again; she wasn't ready to talk about that yet. 'Where's Calder?'

'They took him upstairs, he's being seen by one of our doctors.'

'They roughed him up, Bob.'

'He knew the risks.'

'Even so. He's lost everything, he nearly lost his life.'

'Calder's as tough as they come, he'll be fine.'

'I hope you're right. OK, what now?'

'I thought you might want to rest until Lewis returns?'

'No, I'll wait here until he returns, I mean, what do we do afterwards?'

'We're still figuring all that out.'

The curtain parted just then, and Charlie walked into the room.

'Charlie!' Scarlett gasped, taking her into a fierce hug.

'Hi, Scarlett, glad to see you're OK.'

'How are you?'

'Fine, I'm all lycany now; thanks for the heads up, by the way,' Charlie said sarcastically.

'I'm sorry Charlie, we thought it best to keep that from you as long as we could. I'm so sorry about your gran.'

'Thanks,' Charlie said with a shrug. She didn't want to talk about her gran with Scarlett. 'I guess she agreed with you about keeping all this from me?'

'Yes.'

'You should have trusted us.'

'I see that now.'

'You should have been at the funeral too.'

'I'm sorry about that as well.'

'Seems like you're sorry about a lot of things. Well, you've still to face Lewis on that one.'

'Hello, I'm Scarlett,' Scarlett said, ignoring Charlie's remarks and brushing past her to greet Derek.

'Hello, I'm Derek. I'm not a lycan.'

'Good for you.'

'Derek's been helping us out, he's the resident expert when it comes to ancient places,' Bob said.

'Oh right. I suppose we need to find ancient places now, then?'

'Old railway stations, anyway,' Derek replied.

'Like I said, I'll fill you in later.' Bob said.

Scarlett nodded and sat down again. She felt tired to her bones and every part of her ached. She longed for the peace of a long sleep, but she needed to see her son first.

'We'll leave you to it, I'm sure Bob's got loads to tell you,' Charlie said, escaping into the main shop.

'I'm sure we'll meet again soon,' Derek said, his piercing eyes boring into her.

'Yeah, I'm sure,' Scarlett replied. 'Who the hell is he?' she asked Bob after Derek had disappeared into the shop.

'Someone we picked up along the way. He's been really helpful, even if he is a bit strange.'

'A *bit* strange?'

'OK, a lot strange,' Bob said with a chuckle.

'So, fill me in on what's been happening.'

Bob spent the next hour updating Scarlett on everything that had happened since she'd been gone. She asked a lot of questions and took every opportunity to scold him for putting her son into so much danger. She was struggling to keep her eyes open by the time they'd finished, but perked up when she heard Lewis enter the shop.

'I'll leave you two to it,' Bob said as Lewis walked into the room.

'Mum,' he said coldly, before giving her a quick hug.

'Lewis,' she breathed, desperately trying not to cry.

'How are you feeling?'

'I'm well.'

'They didn't tell me you'd been taken and they were going to rescue you. I would have come with them if I'd known.'

'That's why they didn't. They need to keep you safe.'

'They've not been doing a very good job of that, then.'

'That's what I hear. I'm sorry, son.'

Lewis ignored her apology and sat down. 'You look like you need to rest. We can talk later.'

'No, I need to speak to you now. I need to apologise for leaving you.'

'You did what you thought was best,' he said in a level tone.

'It was a mistake, I'm sorry.'

'Yeah, well, it all worked out in the end.'

'I should have been there for you. I had to go to Edinburgh to look for someone; it's important, but I should have stayed and protected you.'

'That's not what Bob told me, but I'd already gathered he wasn't telling me the whole story. He tends to do that a lot. Did you find who you were looking for?'

'No.'

'I guess they don't have phones in Edinburgh either?'

'I'm sorry, I should have got in touch, but it was difficult.'

'Oh, well, I did a good job without you, anyway.'

'I know, and I'm proud of you.'

'I hear Bob had a spy in The Dark Man's camp. He's full of surprises, that one.'

'Yes, he was the one who rescued me and Calder.'

'Lucky you.'

'I really am sorry.'

'So you keep saying. Look you need rest and I need to update Bob; we can talk tomorrow.' With that he got up and made his way towards the door.

'Yes, we can speak tomorrow,' she shouted after him, but he'd already gone. 'If you want to that is.'

THE PAST IS A FOREIGN COUNTRY

B ob sat down with a sigh. It felt like he'd been on the go for ever. Managing the lycans and the shop, on top of babysitting two argumentative teenagers and coordinating a rescue was taking its toll. He felt wrung out and thin at the edges. Like too little jam spread across too much toast. All he wanted to do was have a drink and an early night, but there was no chance of that now. He sighed once again as he thought about Stan. He knew he was putting his friend in harm's way as soon as he volunteered for the mission, but he told himself there was no alternative. He needed someone in the enemy camp to find out what their plans were. Stan was the ideal candidate. He'd discovered his powers late in life and was an unknown to the lycans and werewolves. He could slip right into their nest and become one of them easily. At least that's what Bob told himself. Stan could pretend he wasn't able to turn just yet, and needed help. That way they wouldn't discover he was really a lycan in disguise. Bob knew they'd be able to smell magic on him and would be curious. It was all going according to plan until

Scarlett had been taken. Or that was what Bob told himself. The reality was that The Dark Man suspected there was a traitor in his camp and took Scarlett and Calder to root him – or her – out. His plan worked perfectly, it seemed. At least he had confirmation that The Dark Man had returned, and if he could, then so could Blaine. Small comfort for the loss of his friend. He only hoped that the other spy he'd managed to secrete into the enemy's camp was safe.

'How did he know, though?' Bob asked himself yet again. 'How did he know there was a traitor? I don't get it.' Bob had told no one about Stan, not Lewis, or Charlie or any of the lycans. There was no way the enemy could have known. 'And how did he know Scarlett was returning?' So many questions left unanswered. Bob hated that. He hated loose ends, and he hated not knowing even more.

'Marco's dead,' Lewis said as he emerged from around a shelf.

'Shit! How?'

Lewis spent the next ten minutes updating Bob on the latest developments and explaining in graphic detail Marco's last moments.

'Another creature with the head of a bull and the body of a man?'

'Yeah a really big man, full of muscles.'

'Sounds like a minotaur, but they're just a myth.' Bob said.

'A myth, really? You can say that after all the magical creatures that have tried to kill us?'

'Yeah, there is that, but I've never heard of anyone meeting one before. Seriously, they're out of a fairy tale book.'

'So is every other creature we've met, Bob. What I want to know is why was it there, and why was it trying to kill us?'

'All good questions.'

'But without any answers, I'm guessing?'

'I'm afraid so.'

'At least we got the swords.'

'How many does that make now?'

'Five.'

'So there're four more still out there.'

'Yeah, but The Gatherer has two, so that leaves two unaccounted for.'

'No, just one. The Dark Man probably has one too and used it to come back into this world.'

'So just one we don't know about. I guess the next step is to get the ones from The Gatherer, then?'

'Yeah, I think so. But that's going to cause mayhem.'

'More like World War Three.'

'We have no choice. We have to stop them.'

'What do we do about Marco's body? The cops will be all over that place by now.'

'Don't worry, we have friends in the constabulary.'

'I bet you do. I'm sorry he's dead. He didn't deserve that; he was only trying to help.' Lewis said, absently picking at a scab.

'You don't seem particularly upset about it?'

'I'm getting used to losing people, I guess,' Lewis replied with a shrug. 'When were you going to tell me the truth about my mum?'

'When she was safe. I'm sorry for keeping that from you.'

'You're good at that. I'm used to you and your secrets, but this is my mum. You should have told me.'

'Yes, I should have, but I didn't want you to worry. I'm sorry.'

Lewis shrugged his shoulders and turned to leave.

'Are we good?' Bob shouted after him.

'Yeah, we're good. Until the next time.'

Bob shook his head and sat down on a window sill. He hated keeping secrets from Lewis, but he had no choice. If he had to, he would do it all again if it meant keeping him and Charlie safe.

'Yeah, you did a bang up job of keeping them safe,' he said to himself. Almost as good a job as he did with his sister.

Bob closed his eyes and winced. He put himself through the pain of remembering at least once a day, even though it

116

had been nearly thirty years.

He'd killed his sister on a glorious sunny day. He remembered there being a cloudless blue sky, topped with a warm yellow sun. There were playing hide and seek in a corn field not too far from their house. Jenny had insisted that he play, even though Bob really wanted to stay in his room and listen to records.

'It's far too nice a day to be indoors and you promised that we could play outside when it was nice.'

He could never resist his sister's demands when she looked at him through her big brown eyes and pushed out her petted lip, the way she did that day.

'Alright, but only for half an hour, I'm going out later.'

'Cool,' Jenny said, a beaming smile splitting her face.

They had gone to the fields and Bob had let her run away, as he counted to one hundred. She took the game seriously, despite only being nine years old, and he knew she'd be searching for a good hiding place. So he didn't peek through his fingers or jump the counting by ten as most big brothers would have done.

'One hundred, coming ready or not!' he shouted at the top of his lungs before setting off in search of her. He crossed the golden field of wheat at a diagonal to start off with, figuring that this was the best way to find her, if she was crouching down in the middle.

There was no sign of her as he made his way across, so he turned left and made his way down one side, then turned and made his way across the field again.

'She's well-hidden this time,' Bob muttered as he reached the opposite side without finding her. He started along the edge of the field once again, trying to see into the dense stalks of wheat as he went. He'd reached halfway when he heard a muffled cry coming from behind the hedge that ran away to his right. Making his way through a small gap in the hedge, he scrambled down the banking on the opposite side, and entered a gully with a small stream running down the middle. The gully was covered by a canopy of trees, that made the air cool and fresh. The family often had picnics there, next to the gurgling stream. But the place was empty today and entering the covering of trees made Bob shiver.

'Jenny?' Bob said, more as a question that a shout.

He heard the muffled cry once again, but this time it seemed to be coming from the trees on the opposite side of the stream. He jumped across and raced into them.

'Are you hiding here?' he said as he rounded the bole of an ancient oak. The sight that greeted him on the other side made his blood run cold. Jenny was sat with her back against the tree, her arms and legs tied in front of her. She had a cloth stuffed into her mouth.

'Jenny!' Bob screamed, diving down in front of her and reaching for her hands. The blow hit him across the back of his head. Before he knew what was happening, he was rolling onto the ground, with stars dancing across his vision.

'So there are two of you, that's helpful,' he heard a voice say from miles away. 'We're going to have way more fun with two.'

'Jenny,' Bob said as he managed to get onto his knees and reach out one hand to his sister.

'Jenny? What a nice name. It's lovely to meet you, Jenny. What a shame that our time together will be so short. I'm going to kill you Jenny, and I bet you don't even know why?'

Jenny started to squirm and thrash against her bonds, her eyes full of terror.

'Don't tremble little one, it will be over soon. I'm one of the nice ones,' the man said, leaning towards Bob's sister and gently brushing her cheek.

'Leave her alone,' Bob managed to squawk.

'And what might your name be? They don't tell me, you see. They just say, Anton, go and kill those lycans, they are evil and need putting into the ground. So Anton goes and kills them, but I would like to know the names of the people I put into the ground, it's only right after all.'

Bob just stared at the man as he tried to clear his head.

'No matter, you're going to die anyway,' Anton said, stepping back. He started to shake and tremble, cracking and breaking sounds coming from his arms and legs, a loud moan of pain escaping from his lips. He fell to the ground and began to writhe around, as hair sprouted from his face.

'What the hell!' Bob shouted, scrambling away from the writhing beast.

The man changed into a large, trembling monster in front of Bob's disbelieving eyes, sending a roar of pain and anger into the air once he'd turned.

Bob wasn't able to comprehend what he was seeing. People didn't simply change into monsters in front of you, not real ones anyway. He heard a muffled cry away to his right and turned to see Jenny still fighting against her bonds. 'Jenny,' he whispered.

The creature turned towards the sound and roared once again, its hot red eyes boring into Bob. It sniffed the air, its massive tongue darting in and out of its mouth, as it tried to lick the fear out of the atmosphere. Then it turned its eyes onto Jenny and roared once again.

'No!' Bob screamed, an electric bolt of terror running through his body. He jumped up and dived between his sister and the monster, stretching out his hands in a desperate attempt to protect her. The electric current rapidly grew inside him until his whole body seemed to hum. He felt his bones crack and break and his skin start to stretch. He let out a scream of pain and terror that turned into a roar, as his mouth extended into a snout and his teeth grew. Falling to the ground, he began to claw and dig at the earth, his mind reeling at what was happening to him. Another wave of pain raced through his body, as his spine cracked then broke, resetting itself as it stretched and grew. In agony, Bob continued to writhe around on the floor, moaning and whimpering as he went.

After a few minutes, the pain subsided and he was left with a feeling of strength and power, the like of which he had never felt. His senses seemed alive. He could smell the grass at his feet, and hear the chirping of birds a mile away. It wasn't long before he became aware of the panting heat of the monster standing a few feet away from him. He looked up to see the creature swaying from side to side, uncertainty spread across its features. With a roar Bob dived at the monster, his newly minted claws spread out, his elongated teeth bared.

The fight was quick and brutal. The creature managed to avoid Bob's first lunge, diving past him and raking its claws down his back as it went. He let out a cry of pain and frustration and dived back at the monster, the contact sending a shudder through the earth and great clods of mud flying into the air. Bob clawed and bit at the creature, lost in blood lust, consumed with beating the opponent in front of him. They rolled and fought around the clearing, Bob snapping and biting at this opponent, until he landed a blow that took the mouth off the creature's face. With a roar of triumph, he dived on the corpse and began to feed, the joy of the kill, and the thrill of the feed racing through his body.

A single thought managed to worm its way into his mind as he ate. The thought of Jenny, still tied and lying on the ground. He turned his head towards his sister, and saw her body lying still. The sight brought him back to himself. He let out a roar of pain, and terror that turned into a scream as he transformed back into a human. Scrambling on all fours he took his sister's lifeless form in his arms and cried into the air. There was a single cut across her neck, a cut clearly caused by his claws.

Bob wiped a tear from his eye as he remembered that day. The pain was still raw for him, despite the years that had gone by. His turning had caused his sister's death, and he could never forgive himself for that. He'd grown silent and introverted after her death, his parents disowning him when they found out what he was, and what he'd done. The only saving grace was that they didn't go to the police. Bob would have been happy if they had, at least he would have paid for his crime. It had been Blaine that had sorted everything, getting rid of the body, taking in a broken and feeble boy, and turning him into the man he was. He was grateful for what Blaine had done, but the price he'd paid ever since had been high.

Bob watched the rain slide gently down the windowpane

120

in front of him and vowed once again to protect Lewis and Charlie. He hadn't been able to protect his sister, even from himself, but he was determined to protect them. With a sigh he turned around and went into the back room for a cup of tea, and to make a phone call to his friend in the police.

THIS IS CALDER ROUGE

Calder moaned as he turned onto his back. He felt as if every part of his body was broken. It hurt to move, it hurt to breathe, it even hurt to open his eyelids. He licked his cracked lips and contemplated reaching out for the glass of water that was at his bedside, but the thought of the pain that would accompany the lifting of his hand made him think again. He didn't know how long he'd lain there in a pain-filled stupor, or when exactly he'd been rescued. The last thing he remembered was the cold floor of the cell, and the pain of the barrel before that.

'Calder,' a voice whispered from the doorway. He only moaned in response. 'Calder, it's me, are you OK?'

'Go away,' he managed to croak.

'I just wanted to make sure you're OK, and to say thank you.'

'What for?' he whispered.

'For being there with me, for coming to get me in the first place. I don't know, just for everything really.'

'No problem, can you get me some water?'

'Of course.' Scarlett hobbled across the room, and picked up the glass. She lifted it to his lips and fed him as gently as she could.

'Are you OK?' he managed to ask once he'd slaked his thirst.

'I think so, I don't know. It wasn't the homecoming I had thought would happen. He's very angry.'

'I would be too.'

'I understand his anger. I abandoned him, but I thought I was doing the right thing.'

'You don't need to convince me.'

'I know, but it helps to talk.'

'Funny, it hurts to talk right now.'

'I'm sorry, I shouldn't have disturbed you; go back to sleep, you need your rest.'

'So what now?'

'What do you mean?'

Calder let out a sigh. It hurt to talk but he needed to hear Scarlett's plans and find out if she was willing to help him.

'You're home. What do you plan to do now?'

'Help him in any way I can.'

'Seems strange that you waited until now to come and help. I'm only saying that's probably what he's thinking.'

'I know, but I made a judgement call, it's that simple.'

'You mean Bob did.'

'No, this was all me.'

'There is a way you can help him.'

'How?'

'Help me. I have a score to settle, and it will hurt The Dark Man if I succeed.'

'You mean with that creature Mono?'

Calder blinked his eyelids in response. He didn't dare move his head just yet.

'What do you have in mind?'

'Mono is The Dark Man's consiglieri. He's lost without him. If we kill him, it will weaken the enemy.'

'Consigla what?'

'His right hand man.'

'Oh, right, but he's a monster. The guy's not human, so

how do we kill him?'

'I'm working on it, but I need your help to convince Bob that going after him is a good idea. He's too wrapped up in these swords and portals. He's taken his eye of the ball, and it's giving them the chance to make their own plans and come after us. We need to strike at them before they can strike at us.'

'I never thought of that.'

Calder just sighed in response. It was the most he'd spoken in a few days, and he was exhausted, but he knew he needed an ally if he was ever to get an opportunity to kill Mono. He took a deep breath and lifted himself up onto his elbows. 'Look, we have to fight them on more than one front. Bob goes for the swords, I go for Mono. It keeps them off balance. Always try and do what your enemy least wants you to do. The Dark Man is weaker without Mono.' He stopped speaking and fell back onto his pillow with a groan.

'OK, just rest. I hear what you're saying. I'll speak to Bob and try to convince him it's a good idea, but you need to come up with a plan. We can't go back to that zoo, that would be suicide. We need to get Mono out into the open. Come up with some ideas and I'll take them to Bob.'

'OK,' Calder gasped, before closing his eyes and falling into a restless sleep, filled with dreams of screaming children and blood soaked cells.

Scarlett sighed and walked out of the room. She wasn't sure what she'd agreed to, but it did make sense to attack the enemy before the enemy attacked them. She was sure she could persuade Bob, as long as Calder came up with a good enough plan. She was glad she'd finally given up the search in Edinburgh and come home. She should have done it sooner, but she couldn't let it go until now. She'd only stopped searching when she was sure he was no longer there. Even so, she knew she still had to find her husband and kill him before he could hurt their son. She smiled as she closed the door behind her. It was good to be in the thick of the action for a change.

A NEW DAWN

The day dawned bright and clear. A thin layer of snow covered the ground, temporarily covering the filth and waste from a thousand discarded packets and cans. Ornate ice patterns formed on broken windows and rusting car bonnets, while a thin white mist seemed to hang in the air like a shroud.

Lewis drew in a cold breath and let it out with a sigh. He loved cold days like this. It felt like the world had been rubbed out, and you got to start all over again. He watched as his white breath curled away into the morning mist, then turned on his heels and entered the shop. They'd all stayed in its many hidden rooms overnight, no one wanting to sleep elsewhere in case The Dark Man and his hordes decided to take revenge for their raid on his lair. He went into the back room and was instantly greeted by the smells of the tea and toast, someone had left on the table.

'Great, I'm starving,' he said to the empty room.

'Save me some,' Charlie said as she entered the room and let out a large yawn.

'Sleep well?' Lewis asked.

'What do you think? I dreamt of werewolves and

demons every time I closed my eyes.'

'Yeah, me too, funny that.'

'I didn't sleep too well either,' Scarlett said as she hobbled into the room.

'That'll be your conscience,' Lewis mumbled under his breath.

'Be nice,' Charlie hissed, kicking him under the table for good measure.

'It's been ages since I had a decent cup of tea. Say what you like about Blaine, he knew his teas.'

'He also knew how to suck the life out of people,' Lewis said.

'Yes, I know, I was only saying,' Scarlett replied with a stutter.

'Yep, he could make a good cup of tea, you can say that for him,' Charlie added, giving Lewis a hard stare.

'So, what are you both up to today?' Scarlett asked after a minute of awkward silence.

'I'm away to search another abandoned railway station, I think,' Charlie answered, 'and I don't know about him. What are you up to, grumpy?'

'Swords.'

'Swords? Is that it? Just swords?'

'We have four more to get.'

'Any clues about where they are?' Scarlett asked.

'The Gatherer has two and The Dark Man has one. We think another demon is out and about, so that's the fourth one.'

'Oh, well, easy then,' Scarlett said with a laugh.

'Yeah, dead easy,' Lewis said, shaking his head.

'Perhaps I could give you a hand? I was always handy with a sword,' Scarlett said brightly.

'It's fine, we've got it covered.'

'You could come with me, I could use the help,' Charlie offered.

'Thanks,' Scarlett replied with a thin smile.

'Morning, troops, how are we all this fine morning?' Bob asked as he entered the room.

'You're in a good mood, what are you up to?' Charlie asked.

'Nothing; can't I just be in a good mood?'

'No, it usually means danger and death.'

'Ye of little faith. For your information, I slept well last night and woke up with the smell of victory in my nostrils.'

'Told you he was up to something. Spit it out,' Charlie said with a scowl.

'We need to make war on The Gatherer. Best do it today and strike while the iron's hot.'

'Is that all? Here I was thinking you were planning something really dangerous,' Charlie said.

'You can't be serious?' Scarlett asked.

'I don't see any other way of getting the swords he's got, do you?'

'We could talk to him. He has a price for everything,' Scarlett suggested.

'The swords won't be for sale, trust me.'

'So, you just plan on walking through an army of magical creatures, hold The Gatherer at knife point and take the swords? If you can even find them in that heap of rubbish he surrounds himself with.' Lewis asked.

'Yep, unless you can come up with a better plan?'

'You did wake up in a good mood today. We're all going to die,' Lewis said.

'Why go for them first, what about the other two?' Charlie asked.

'The Dark Man has an army behind him, and we have no idea where the fourth sword is. Besides, you need to concentrate on finding the portals. It's no good having one without the other.'

'We have two already, and I bet The Gatherer is sitting on one,' Charlie suggested.

'That still leaves six.'

'They're no good without the swords,' Charlie said.

'That we know of. We can't be sure, so we need to know where they are. Be prepared and all that,' Bob replied.

'I never took you for a boy scout,' Scarlett said with a

chuckle.

'You have no idea.'

'I know we need those swords, but we need a better plan than just walking up to him and demanding he gives them up,' Charlie said grumpily.

'I might have an idea,' Calder said from the doorway.

'You should be in bed,' Scarlett said.

'I'm fine. Being half magic makes me a very quick healer.' Even so, Calder sat down carefully.

'What's your idea?' Bob asked.

'Attack.'

'Attack, is that it?'

'What do you think The Gatherer fears more than anything else?' Calder asked.

'Soap and water,' Lewis said.

'No, his brothers,' Calder said, ignoring Lewis's sarcastic response.

'Why would he fear them?' Lewis asked.

'He's been in that hole for years. Until now, I think he's been protected by Blaine. It suited Blaine to leave him where he was. One less portal to close, one less demon to deal with. But Blaine's gone and there's no one to stop them coming through, apart from us.'

'So, you think he'll do a deal?' Charlie asked hopefully.

'No, he's a hoarder and won't give up the things he's got, unless he has no choice.'

'I still don't see how we can make him give us the swords,' Lewis said.

'We can't, but maybe bringing in The Dark Man can.'

'How?' Lewis asked.

'With a little bit of chaos. The Dark Man has no interest in his brothers, apart for Blaine, or he would have taken on The Gatherer years ago. We know he wants Lewis and Charlie. Why don't we entice him into Victoria Station, and kill two birds with one stone? The chaos of a fight with the Dark Man will give us the opportunity to deal with The Gatherer as well. It will also stop all those magical creatures from coming to his rescue, when we attack him too.'

'That's crazy, but it might actually work.' Bob mused.

'How do we get him there?' Lewis asked.

'We send him a message of course.'

'Of course.'

'We're going to need Charlie as well as Lewis for that fight, that means no searching for the portals,' Bob said.

'Yes, this has to be our priority. We get the swords, then we can take our time looking for the portals.' Lewis said.

'You changed your tune quick. A minute ago, searching for the portals was a priority,' Charlie said.

'Yeah well, priorities can change,' Lewis said.

'Clearly. Oh no, does that mean I don't get Derek's wonderful company, how will I cope?' Charlie asked, with a grin spread across her face.

'He can come too,' Bob said, with a grin.

'Super.'

'Wait a minute, you're talking about taking on two demons and an army of werewolves, not to mention God knows how many magical creatures, all of whom will be upset that we have raided their magical watering hole. This is madness, you're going to get a lot of people killed. There has to be a better way, a safer way.' Scarlett said.

'Don't worry, we've been taking care of ourselves for a while now,' Lewis said.

Scarlett looked at him with a cold stare, then turned to Bob. 'There has to be a safer way to get those swords.'

'I can't think of one, can you? Most of the magical creatures will run as soon as the fighting starts. The Gatherer won't have any fighters when they leave, apart from that two-headed dog and the filthy gatekeeper, and I know for a fact they're cowards. We just need to worry about the werewolves, and we know how to deal with them.' Bob said.

'And The Dark Man?' Scarlett asked.

'He only has Mono, and I can take care of him,' Calder said ominously.

'Besides, Lewis defeated him last time, he can do it again,' Bob said.

Scarlett shook her head, but kept her mouth closed. She

could see that Calder wanted to flush out Mono and get his revenge, but she didn't think he would try and get them to take on The Dark Man as well.

'So how do we let The Dark Man know?' Charlie asked.

'Jillian Lightfoot,' Bob said.

'Who?' Charlie and Lewis asked in unison.

'Someone I spoke to a few days ago, she's just returned from abroad.'

'Who is she, and how can she take a message to the demon?' Lewis asked.

'She's an angel, if you must know.'

'Seriously, who is she Bob?' Lewis said, shaking his head.

'What, you can believe in demons but not angels? She's a messenger from God, so I think she'll be the ideal person to take a message for us.'

'You're not joking, are you?'

'No, I'm not; she'll take the message for us.'

The group sat in silence, taking in what Bob had just said.

'So God exists?' Lewis said, half to himself.

'Yep, and she's pissed apparently.'

'I bet, she's made a right pigs ear of the world.' Charlie said.

'I don't think she sees it that way.' Bob said.

'She's a she?' Lewis asked with a shake of his head.

'Yep, you couldn't trust a man to make this lot.'

'OK, enough of this existential stuff. What message do we want to send.?' Scarlett said.

'Simple, we're waiting for you at the station, come and get what you've always wanted.' Bob said.

'You think he'll go for that?'

'Why not? I would,' Lewis said.

'OK, I'll get in touch with Jillian,' Bob said, standing up.

'Hang on, it can't be as simple as that?' Scarlett said.' He's going to need more than a message telling him to be there at such and such a time, no one's that stupid.'

'Yep, you're right, that's why we give him a sword.'

'Are you mental?' Lewis shouted. 'We can't give him a sword.'

'I'll give one to Jillian, she can show him then bring it back.'

'He'll just take it from her.' Lewis said.

'She's more powerful than you think, and besides, even a demon isn't stupid enough to go up against God.'

'I don't think he'll fall for that; it's a bit obvious,' Lewis said, unconvinced.

'Fear is always a motivation. We tell him that we're going for the two swords The Gatherer has, and this is proof that we have more. There's no way he can ignore that. He'll have to go after them as well.'

'Yeah, that could work,' said Charlie, 'as long as you can trust this Jillian?'

'We can trust her,' Bob reassured them.

'OK, then it looks like we have a plan,' Lewis said, reluctantly.

At that they all stood up.

'Charlie, you go and get the troops ready, and give them the good news about The Dark Man's return,' said Bob.

'They'll be thrilled,' Charlie replied sarcastically.

'Lewis, go and get a sword. Calder, start thinking about the message we want Jillian to send and I'll get in touch with her.'

'What about me?' Scarlett asked.

'The dishes need doing,' Lewis said.

'You're coming with me,' Bob said, ignoring Lewis. 'I don't want you out of my sight.'

RUMBLES IN THE DEEP

D erek rocked back and forth in his chair, his mind a confusing cloud of images and sounds. He remembered being at the shop and being more afraid than he'd ever been in his life, but after that the world had gone dark, like he'd fallen into a deep river and been swept along on its currents. He'd risen to the surface every now and again to see a face or hear a sound, only to fall back into its depths.

Derek had always been in complete control of his faculties. He never drank alcohol, and the idea of taking drugs made him gag. He didn't like coffee because it made him feel too racy, and he avoided taking too much sugar for the same reason. The idea that he could lose an entire afternoon and not remember getting home terrified him to his core.

He'd come to his senses sitting on the edge of the settee in his living room, and had stayed there ever since, gently rocking back and forth as his mind jumped from one terror to another. He'd reached for his phone several times, thinking of phoning Jamie or someone else from Abandoned Glasgow, but he didn't know what he would say, and he was certain they'd remove him as Chair of the group the minute they found out he was losing his mind. There was no way he could let that happen.

After an age, he got up and walked to the window. It was dark outside, the street empty of traffic and pedestrians. A single street lamp sent a pale glow across the pavement, and into his garden. Derek felt more alone than at any time in his life, and his mind wandered to his dead girlfriend, as it had done on so many occasions since her death.

'Do you miss me, my love?' a quiet voice asked from the other side of the room.

'You're not real,' Derek said without turning around.

'Oh, but I am, my love. You made me real. You called out to me in the darkness, and I answered. Our love can even conquer death.'

'You're just a broken bit of my mind,' Derek whimpered.

'Yes, my love, I am in your mind and in your soul. Didn't you know that you can never leave me?'

'You're not real,' Derek said with force.

'Turn around and look at me, my love, see how real I am.'

Despite himself, Derek turned around to see a terrifying vision stood in front of him. It was his Cindy, but it wasn't. Like before she seemed to glow with an ethereal light and her eyes were jet black. Her lips were curled into a cruel smile that the real Cindy would never have been able to make.

'You're not her,' Derek said breathlessly.

'I am her and more, my love. I'm everything you've ever wanted me to be, she didn't look at you the way I do, or touch herself like this.' At that the creature grabbed her breasts and started to rub them.

'Stop it!' Derek shouted, turning away.

'Why, you know you want to?'

'Go away, I don't want you here.'

'Very well, but someone else will come in my place, someone who's desperate to meet you, but I don't think you'll want to meet him.'

There was silence for a few minutes, but Derek didn't dare turn around. He knew Cindy had gone and something else had replaced her, something far more sinister.

'Aren't you going to look at me, Derek?' a voice hissed into the room. Derek whimpered and began to shake. The sound was only a whisper, but it drilled down into Derek's soul, making him shiver all over. Despite himself, he turned around.

A thin man with hawk-like features stood in front of him, his eyes the colour of hot coals. He was dressed in a jet-black suit and black shirt, open at the neck. His dark hair was razor straight. When he smiled, he revealed dazzling white teeth.

'That's better,' he said slowly, 'I thought it best we meet in person, so to speak.'

'What do you want?' Derek managed to ask.

'I've already got what I want from you, Derek. I've got your soul.'

'What!' Derek gasped.

'You gave it to me willingly in the shop, don't you remember? Oh well, I'm sure it will come back to you – the memory, not the soul.'

'There's no such thing as a soul.'

'Well, not for you anymore,' the man said, laughing.

'If you've got what you want, why do you need to meet me?'

'I have *what* I want from you, but not *everything* I want. I need your help, you see.'

'Why should I help you?'

'A good question. I'm sure by now you know what I am?'

Derek nodded.

'Good, that will save time. Now you know what I am, you'll also know that I like a bargain, so here's mine. If you help me, I'll give you back your soul. You'll be square with the man, as they say.'

'Why should I believe you; everyone knows you're the prince of lies?'

'A very good question, but what have you got to lose? You've already lost everything that you can. Nice work with Cindy, by the way, she was very annoying. Yes, I know I could simply take over your body and do my own dirty work, but this particular job is delicate, and I don't want them to see me coming.'

'What do you want me to do?'

'It's as easy as falling off a log. I want you to introduce me to someone.'

'Is that it?'

'Yep, easy peasy, lemon squeezy.'

'Surely you can do that yourself?'

'Well, yes and no. As I said, it's delicate. I need to speak to someone, and I don't want them to see me coming, so I have to give you control for a bit, and that should do the trick.'

'You've possessed me, haven't you?'

'Of course I have, Derek, and it's been real fun. You are just my kind of guy. Now I need you to do this thing for me, and that will be the end of our adventure.'

'Who is it?'

'My son, the Price of the Blood himself.'

'Lewis, he's your son?'

'The very same.'

'But why do you need me to introduce you? If you've possessed me, you can just go up to him.'

'Yes and no, I need to speak to him as myself , not through you. Look it's complicated, just do as I ask and all will be well.'

Derek sat down and shook his head. His emotions were running wild; not only had he lost control but he'd been possessed. How was he supposed to cope with that fact?

'Can you hear them, Derek? Can you hear the drums?'

'What?'

'There are drums in the deep, heralding the arrival of my brothers. I can stop them, but I need your help, will you help me?'

The confused and frightened man, who was half sure

he'd gone insane, could only nod.

'Good, this will be such fun,' the man said with a bright smile.

NOT SO MERRY A MEETING

Jillian stood in front of them with a frown spread across her brow. 'You want me to tell him what?'

'That we're going to get the swords from The Gatherer, and then we're coming for him,' Bob said casually.

'You do remember the conversation we had just a few days ago?'

'Of course I do.'

'And you remember what I told you about the boss? How she wants you to stop?'

'Yes, I particularly remember that.'

'So why do you think I'd help you to make things worse?'

'Because it will make things better in the long run.'

'So you say, but you can't be sure of that and innocents will die once again.'

'Not innocents, just werewolves.'

'What about all those creatures that hang around in the station?'

'They'll leave as soon as the trouble starts.' The fact that the trouble was normally started by some of those creatures had escaped Bob, but no one bothered to mention it to him.

Jillian sighed and sat down. 'I'm sorry, but I can't help you.'

'This is the chance to end it all, can't you see that? We know what their weaknesses are. If we get the swords, we can kill them. It will put an end to the war, an end to all the suffering and an end to their ambitions on earth. We can finally live in peace.'

'Too many innocents have died already, didn't you hear about the guy who was killed in the museum the other night? He wasn't a lycan or a werewolf, he was a human. Some magical creature killed him, and it didn't sound like it was one of your enemies either, so what peace will you bring if you kill the demons?'

Lewis shifted uncomfortably in his seat but didn't say anything.

'I'm not saying people don't die, that happens every day, but surely even you can admit that stopping the demons taking over earth is a good thing?' Bob said.

'Some of them have been here for millennia, and I don't see the earth on fire.'

'It's only a matter of time,' Calder said.

'It's different this time,' Scarlett piped up,' I heard them talking when I was their captive; now Blaine's gone The Dark Man is planning to take over. He doesn't just want to feed, he wants to bathe in blood and fire. Bob's right, we have to stop them before the earth as we know it is gone for good. I don't think your boss will want that either.'

Jillian shook her head and sighed once again. 'Even if I take your message, and that lovely sword as evidence, how do you know he'll turn up?'

'We'll all be there, me, Charlie, Bob, the whole crew,' Lewis said. 'He won't be able to resist and besides, he can't chance us getting those other swords, it's far too dangerous for him.'

Jillian nodded and pursed her lips. 'You're only going after the swords and the werewolves, nothing else?'

'The Dark Man, obviously,' Lewis said.

'Him as well?'

'Yes, but that's all,' Bob answered.

'Alright, I'll help you, but this has to be it.'

'Once we get the swords and kill the demons or close the portals, whatever way works best.'

'I always knew you'd make me side with you,' she said to Bob, shaking her head.

'So did I, we're the good guys remember?'

'If you like. I just hope she sees it that way.'

'Well, if she's everywhere she already knows and in fact she made the decision for us, isn't that right?' Charlie asked.

'Don't be smart.' Jillian warned her.

'Wouldn't dream of it.'

'When are you going to the station?'

'This afternoon, strike while the iron's hot. Besides, we don't want to give him any time to plan.'

'I'd better get going then,' Jillian said, standing up, taking the sword and straightening her coat.

'How will we know that the message has been delivered?' Lewis asked.

'It will be, you can count on that,' she said, giving both Lewis and then Scarlett a hard stare.

'Yes, but...'

'It will be,' Bob interrupted him.

Lewis nodded and held his tongue, he didn't trust this Jillian any more than he believed she was an angel sent from God; there were some things even he couldn't believe.

They quietly went their separate ways after Jillian left. Charlie went to her room while Bob and Scarlett went for a cup of tea. Calder staggered into the back room with them, leaving Lewis alone in the shop. The lycans were either out on patrol or sleeping off last night's exertions.

He sighed to himself and sat on the windowsill, a pale light bathing him in its glow. He knew he should go back and speak to his mum, but he was still angry at her. If he was being honest, he was seething. Whatever excuse she'd given he couldn't believe she would just abandon him. He remembered how he met Bob. It was a chance encounter and his mum had already left, so how could she have been sure that Bob and the rest would look after him and Charlie? Who abandons their child to a bunch of magical creatures?

Lewis had always been close to his mum. That's what hurt him the most, the fact that she'd walked away without saying a word, and left him to deal with Blaine and the demons. What did it say about how she really felt, that she'd run away without second's thought?

'Am I disturbing you?'

Lewis jumped at the words and whirled around, ready to fight.

'I'm sorry, I didn't mean to startle you,' Derek said stepping back.

'Derek,' Lewis said breathlessly, 'you shouldn't sneak up on people like that.'

'I didn't, you were lost in your thoughts. I've been stood here for a few minutes.'

'Yeah, well, what do you want?'

Derek tilted his head and stared at Lewis. 'Someone wants to meet you,' he said.

'Here I am, tell them to come say hello.'

'They're already here.'

'What are you talking about?'

'Over there by the shelves,' Derek said, pointing to his right.

Lewis followed Derek's hand and saw a shadowy figure standing in the gloom between the shelves. The room suddenly felt cold, even the pale light from the window shed no warmth.

'Who is that?' Lewis asked just above a whisper.

'Go over and find out but hurry, we don't have long.'

Swallowing hard, Lewis rose from the windowsill and made his way over to the figure. At first he thought he might be dreaming, that he had fallen asleep while staring out at the street, but the beating of his heart and the prickly feeling racing across his skin, told him he was not.

'Who are you?' he asked, stopping just short of the

gloom.

'I think you know who I am.' The figure stepped forward to reveal the sharp features and piercing eyes of a man. Lewis gasped and took a step backwards.

'You're me,' he stammered.

'Yes and no,' the man responded. 'Surely she's told you about me?'

'Who?'

'Your mother.'

'Why would she?' Lewis stammered, but he already knew the answer.

'Because I'm your father,' the man replied.

'You're a demon,' Lewis said, his heart sinking as he realised the truth.

'Yes. I thought she'd have told you, but never mind. That's how princes are made.'

'You're a liar.'

'Of course I am, but there are some things even I don't need to lie about. Ask her, I'm sure she'll tell you the truth.'

'What do you want?'

'To meet you, to talk, nothing more.'

'Another lie.'

'It's my right after all, you are my blood.'

'You're nothing to me,' Lewis responded, his anger rising.

'You cannot deny the truth, my son. I may not have been the dad you always wanted, but I am him nevertheless.'

'You're no father of mine. A quick roll in the hay doesn't make you a parent.'

'I'm so much more than that. Search your memories Lewis. I didn't abandon you. I left to save you.'

'Everyone's been telling me that lately. Now I hear it from a demon I've only just met.'

'You must remember, my son. I was with you for a long time, I was your dad for a long time when you were little.'

'I have no memory of you, that makes you a liar.'

'No, it means your memories have been tampered with. I was there when you were born, I was there for your first birthday and everyday in-between. I remember your first tooth and your first steps. Don't you remember the park we used to go to with the swings? You loved the swings.'

Lewis took a step back; he did remember a park and bright red swings. He loved to sit on them and be pushed up into the air. But it was his mum behind him, not this creature.

'What about your teddy? You loved that teddy. You called him Ted, it was your first word. Don't you remember the big blue bow he wore, or his bright shiny eyes? We had to put him in the washing machine at night while you were sleeping. You couldn't bear to be parted from him for a second.'

Lewis trembled at the memories. How could this creature know about Ted, or the play park?

'You're reading my mind,' he stammered.

'Don't be silly, you're far too powerful for that, not like that weak minded fool over your shoulder. You know it's true. I was there, I never abandoned you.'

'Even if it is true, you haven't been around for years. That's abandonment in my book.'

'How could I stay to watch you grow up? If my brothers knew the truth, they would stop at nothing to have you, to take your powers then rip you limb from limb.'

'So you left to protect me; that was convenient.'

'No, I didn't. You must remember the car? We were being chased, you were asleep in the back, but we crashed. I had to leave you and your mum then. They couldn't find me with you, that would have been the death of all of us.'

Lewis felt weak at the knees, he did remember the car and the crash. He remembered waking up at the bottom of a deep well, climbing out and racing across the field in terror.

'There were red eyes,' he stammered. 'I remember the red eyes.'

'Yes, they were chasing us. They would stop at nothing to catch us.' The demon moved in close as he spoke, putting his hand gently on Lewis's shoulder.

'They are the real demons,' he said, 'All I wanted to do was protect you and your mum. You were my family, my loves.'

'How did you get here?' Lewis asked, shaking his head to clear his increasingly clouded mind.

'You know how. I came through a portal.'

'How, tell me about it?'

The demon stepped back, temporarily put off balance. He hadn't expected these types of questions.

'St Enoch's,' he said after a pause. 'I came through a while ago; my followers finally found my sword and brought me through. You know all about the swords?'

'Yes. So you'd been sent back to hell, then?'

'Yes,' the demon replied with a hiss. 'Blaine found me and sent me back. He had that power, but he didn't know about you. At least, I don't think he knew I was your father.'

'Did it hurt, coming back from hell?'

'No, it was a joy. All the pain disappears when we come into this realm; why do you think we want to stay here? The air is sweet and the water fine,' he said with a wry smile. 'It is my portal, my very own. A simple bit of blood and I am home.'

'Who died to let you through?'

'I don't know,' his father replied with a shrug. 'It was a willing sacrifice, it has to be. Once they are gone, they are free and so are we.'

Lewis sighed and shook his head.

'Is that the only way you can come through?'

'No, there are other ways, but they are hard,'

Lewis's mind had been churning ever since his father has appeared. He was asking questions as much to buy time and clear his head, as he was to get information.

'I always wanted to return to you and your mum, you have to believe that,' the demon said, moving in close. 'I miss saying good night and reading you a bedtime story. I miss taking you to the sweetie shop, and the zoo. You remember the zoo? You loved the monkeys. They took so much from us that night. We crashed into a field, and they came after us. I wanted to stay, but they would have killed us all if I had. You have to remember, son, you have to remember that I was there, that I was your father then and now,' the demon said, moving in close once again, and resting his hand on Lewis's shoulder.

Lewis felt his mind grow foggy as he tried to remember the car and the chase. It had been late at night. He'd been so tired he hadn't been able to keep his eyes open. He remembered the soft seat and snuggling into its warmth. He remembered the hum of his parents' conversation, then their harsh whispers of desperation. The car had flown high into the air, sending him rattling around and then down into the well beneath the seats. This was what saved him, although he only realised it now. Now that he knew this was all real, that his father was real, and a demon. He looked up into his father's piercing eyes. He was so close that he could smell the mint from his breath and the cream in his hair.

'What do you want?' he managed to stammer, his legs feeling like lead, his arms as heavy as girders.

'To be a family again, that's all. That's not too much to ask for, is it? his father purred.

Lewis shook his head, not sure he could speak anymore. It felt like the world was a million miles away, that he was being carried on a cloud to soft and dreamless sleep. 'I need to sit down,' he mumbled.

'Yes, that would be best, let's all have a rest. We can catch up later.'

Lewis felt himself spiralling downwards until his knees hit the floor. His head felt too heavy for his neck, and his arms were now so heavy he couldn't lift them off the floor. If he could just sleep for ten minutes, he'd feel better, he told himself.

'That's it, just sleep,' he heard his dad say from a million miles away.

'Yeah, just sleep,' he mumbled. What a strange thing it was for his dad to turn up like that, and after all those years. His dad who loved him and just wanted them to be a family. His dad who'd took him to the swing park and looked after his teddy. His dad who loved him, his dad who was a demon.

'A demon,' he sighed as he slipped into the edge of

sleep.

A demon! his mind roared.

Lewis's eyes flew open just in time to see his dad lean in towards him, his mouth open wide, his teeth bared.

'No!' he screamed, pushing his father away from him.

Rage boiled through his veins. The creature was getting ready to eat him while he slept. His father was going to eat him. He turned in a heartbeat and lunged at the demon.

They crashed backwards into a shelf, a ball of raging violence that sent objects flying and glass crashing around them.

Lewis snarled and snapped at the demon, but the creature fought back, smashing a vase into the side of his head and sending him sprawling.

'Lewis, wait!' the creature shouted, but it was too late, all Lewis wanted to do was rip the demon apart. He lunged forward and hit the creature full in the chest. The force of the impact smashing them both through the front window and out into the street.

Lewis felt a thousand tiny cuts bite into his skin as he rolled across the road and came to a stop in a furry heap. He was disorientated for a few seconds before he shook his head clear and rose onto his haunches, shards of glass falling off him like raindrops.

'You have to stop this before you bring too much attention to yourself,' his father said to him from the other side of the street.

Lewis rose to his full height, the rage churning inside him once again. He prepared to launch himself at his prey, but stopped when he looked over at his father. He held Derek by the neck, a long thin blade resting lightly against the side of his head.

'I will plunge this blade into his brain if you don't stop,' his father said.

Lewis changed back into a human as Bob and Charlie came running out of the shop.

'What the hell's going on!' Bob demanded.

'Hello Bob, long time no see. I was just having a

fatherly chat with my son.'

'What the hell do you want?' Bob demanded.

'Just to talk, nothing more.'

'Liar!' Lewis screamed. 'He was going to eat me.'

'No, not eat you, I was going to share your essence, that's all.'

'You were going to eat me.'

'You were trying to take what isn't yours,' Bob said.

'He's my son, I have the right.'

'You have no right!' Lewis shouted.

'I'll die without it.'

'Good, one less demon in the world,' Bob replied.

The demon sighed then slid the knife into Derek's ear. He went stiff and let out a groan, before tumbling to the floor.

Lewis gasped and rushed to Derek's side. He lay cold and lifeless on the ground, a small trickle of blood dripping from his ear.

'I'll kill you!' Lewis hissed, but his father had disappeared.

ACE IN THE HOLE

Beth sat down with a sigh. She'd been on her feet all day, patrolling around and around the perimeter of the zoo.

'What's wrong with you?' Norman asked gruffly. He was the head of her unit, and a real pain in her arse.

'Nothing, just tired.'

'Don't let Mr Mono hear you say that. He'll give you double guard duty.'

'I don't get it, they know where we are, why haven't they attacked?' Beth asked, the frustration clear in her voice.

'Eager to kill lycans, are you? Don't worry, you'll get your chance. They haven't attacked because they don't have the numbers. We're more powerful than them, and this is our ground. They'd be crazy to attack us here. I hope you're right and they do. Lycan flesh is sweet,' Norman said, licking is lips.

Beth swallowed hard and tried to hide her revulsion. 'I'll go for another circuit.'

'You do that.'

She left the room and started to walk slowly towards the perimeter of the zoo, feeling a sense of relief now that she was away from her revolting commander, and out in the clear air. She'd been a part of The Dark Man's army since before he'd been sent back to hell. Another spy Bob had managed to put in place under Mono's nose. Beth felt she was being watched every minute, and half expected to be ripped apart by werewolves after they uncovered Stan, her fellow spy. But all The Dark Man and his captains has done was to congratulate themselves on finding a spy in their midst, never considering for a second that there was more than one.

'Penny for your thoughts.'

Beth jumped back and was halfway through her turning when she saw who it was.

'Oh, my God, don't do that!' she gasped, turning back into a human, and trying desperately to cover up the fact that her eyes had remained the cold blue of a lycan as she'd begun to turn. Like Stan she'd been given strong contacts by Bob to hide her eye colour, but she'd left her spares back at her bunk.

'Sorry, I've been standing here for a while, you were miles away.'

'Yeah, well, I've got a lot on my mind.'

'I bet. It must be hard to decide if you should go clockwise of anti-clockwise around the perimeter.'

'Very funny. What are you doing out here anyway?'

'Looking for you, the boss wants to see you.'

'Mono wants to see me, why?' Beth asked, her stomach dropping.

'How do I know? I just do what I'm told. You best be quick, you know how he doesn't like to be kept waiting.'

Beth nodded and with a sigh, began to make her way to Mono's office. It had been the office of the zoo manager in times gone past, and everyone agreed it was the coldest part of the place. Whether or not that was circumstance, or the effect of Mono living there, no one knew.

Beth approached the black door with trepidation. She had no idea why Mono would want to see her. As far as she knew, he considered her to be just another grunt werewolf. Cannon fodder to be used during a fight. That was just the way she wanted it. The fact he'd asked for her left a feeling of dread in the pit of her stomach. What if he'd found out what she really was? She was sure he could make her suffer in ways she couldn't imagine. Beth set her face into what she hoped was a blank mask and knocked on the door.

'Come.'

She opened the door and felt a wave of cold air hit her. She tried not to shiver, but felt a tremor run down her spine as she entered the room.

'Here she is,' Mono said in a flat tone, devoid of any emotion.

'Good afternoon, Beth,' a soft voice said. Beth turned to see a woman standing by the window. She was small, with shocking white hair, and the coldest blue eyes Beth had ever seen.

'Good afternoon,' she replied with a stammer.

'This is Jillian Lightfoot, an angel,' Mono said. 'She needs a female werewolf and you will fit the bill.'

'How can I help?' Beth asked, recovering her composure.

'We need you for a very special mission,' the angel replied. 'One that requires you to be inconspicuous, can you do that?'

'I can try.'

'Good, you're just what we're looking for, I think. We're all about to go to Victoria Station. The Royal Prince and Princess will be there, and they have challenged The Dark Man to meet them. To end the war, once and for all.'

'As if they can,' Mono said flatly. 'They are going for The Gatherer's sword and apparently he has Blaine's as well. They have sent this angel with this one as evidence of their intent.' Mono said, nodding down to the gold and silver sword the stranger held in her hand.

'What exactly do you want me to do?' Beth asked.

'Kill the Prince,' the angel replied.

'What! I can't, he's all powerful, I'll never be able to get close enough to him to try,' Beth said, gasping at the idea.

'You can and you will,' Mono said. 'He will be

distracted during the fight, we'll make sure of that. We'll give you the opportunity to get close and kill him.'

'How can I kill him?'

'With this,' Jillian said, holding out the sword she held in her hand. 'This sword is the only thing that can kill a demon on this world, but what the lycans don't know is that they are the only things that can kill the magic of a Prince of the Blood as well.'

'Why would you want to kill him, isn't he our food source?'

'He's one of them,' Mono replied, 'but there are others, and you ask too many questions. This is an order from The Dark Man, you can obey, or you can die, choose.' Mono stepped into Beth's space and grabbed her arms. He leant in until their faces were inches apart, their noses touching. Beth smelt the strong smell of engine oil and damp radiating from him and something else, far in the background. At first she didn't know what it was then it struck her, she'd smelt it before. It was the aroma of something that had been dead for a long time. Something that had gone beyond decay, and was now a dried empty husk. The smell terrified her.

'Look at me.'

Beth obeyed, staring into the black pits that should have shown life but only displayed despair and loss. They were the eyes of a monster, eyes that had seen millennia of death and pain, eyes that had seen the rise and fall of civilisations. She felt herself floating away, falling into the dark pools.

'You will do as ordered. You will kill the Prince of the Blood.'

'I obey,' Beth said slowly, her voice sounding a million miles away.

'Good, now go with the angel, she will take you to the station and get you in place.'

Air rushed into Beth's lungs, cold as ice. She looked around the room as if seeing it for the first time. Mono and Jillian stood watching her, waiting to see what she would do next. She nodded and turned towards Lightfoot, following her out of the door.

Raking Through the Ashes

Jamie sighed as he scanned the empty room. Cindy and Marco were dead, Derek too. The members of Abandoned Glasgow were dying quicker than mayflies.

'And they only last a day,' Jamie said to himself.

He sat in sad solitude and wondered where to start. Bob had called him earlier to give him the news that Derek was dead, and the only thing he could think to do was come to his house check on his much loved treasures. He didn't expect to get in, but the door had been unlocked. The room felt empty and sombre now its master had gone. The light shining through the window was pale and weak, casting everything in a cold glow. Derek's hoard, so lovingly assembled against the back wall, seemed like a collection of fool's gold to Jamie. All it had brought his friends was death and tragic loss to the rest of the group. What would happen to Abandoned Glasgow now? Jamie supposed there would be an election and he would become Chair. He could hear Derek's complaints. 'You're not ready for such a responsibility,' he would say, 'you don't know where the best places are, where the true treasure is.'

'What about you Derek?' Jamie asked the room. 'How did knowing the best places work out for you?'

Jamie felt a surge of anger course through him as he contemplated the wasteful loss of his friends. He jumped up and rushed to the back wall, grabbing the first thing that came to hand and flinging it across the room. The porcelain plate shattered against the wall, sending shards bouncing across the floor. In a rage Jamie reached for the next thing and the next. Throwing each one behind him as he grabbed for another. A cacophony of breaking treasures filled the room, each one bearing the face of its lost master.

'What a waste!' Jamie shouted as he reached for the next treasure and threw it behind him.

The floor quickly became littered with broken artefacts. A cog from a large machine came to rest next to a pocket watch. They were joined by a broken washing board and half a porcelain bed pan. Jamie eventually reached Derek's pride and joy, his collection of railway signs. Each one got the same treatment until they were all lying in a heap in the middle of the floor. When he reached the back wall, Jamie looked up and halted. A small painting of a large tree, previously hidden behind other artefacts, was now visible. What made him pause was the fact that the tree was depicted growing inside an enormous cavern. The painting was out of place next to iron and steel, but this wasn't what struck Jamie as odd, it was the tree itself that made him wonder. It seemed to sway as if the wind was blowing through its branches and he was sure that the bark was changing colour before his eyes.

'Who grows a tree inside a cave,' he mused to himself.

'Who indeed,' a voice said from behind him.

Jamie jumped at the sound and stumbled over broken bits of artefacts until he fell to the ground in a heap.

'You have to be careful, young Jamie, Abandoned Glasgow can be dangerous to your health.'

A pale hand reached out into Jamie's eye line. It seemed to shimmer as if covered in silver. Without knowing why, Jamie shivered, but he reached for it anyway and the shiver changed to a rattle as the cold contact ran through him. He was pulled to his feet and immediately came face to face with a wide smile and sharp eyes, the colour of dying embers.

'Let's see if we can't keep you alive for a little while longer, what do you say?'

'Who are you?'

'A friend of your late Chairman, or should it be Chairperson in these enlightened times?'

'Really, he never mentioned you?'

'There's a lot that Derek never mentioned. Like the fact he killed Cindy, did you know that?'

'It was an accident.'

'Yes, well, that's what he told you, anyway.'

'I'm sorry, but who are you?' Jamie insisted, with as much force as his shaking body could muster.

'I told you, I'm a friend.'

'Well, what are you doing here?'

'Derek very kindly offered to look after something for me, I'm simply retrieving my artefact.'

Jamie doubted that Derek would have offered to look after anything, for anyone, especially this strange person in front of him, but a part of his mind was screaming at him to take care.

'Oh, I see,' he replied nonchalantly, 'well, maybe I can help, what was it?'

'Ah, Jamie, that would be telling. After all, I trusted Derek with my item, no one else.'

'Derek's dead, maybe I can help?'

'Maybe you can; after all, you have been searching through his things already.'

'Yeah, well, I … erm …' Jamie replied, stumbling over his word.

'Don't get me wrong, I totally understand your anger. He was a bit of a fool, wasn't he?' the stranger asked, with a sly wink.

'What is it you need?' Jamie replied, his anger starting to rise. Derek wasn't even in his grave yet and this man was already insulting his memory.

'Perhaps I can trust you,' the man said to himself, rubbing his chin thoughtfully. 'It's a very important treasure, perhaps the most important Derek has ever held. Something so important people have died for it,' the man said, moving closer.

Jamie stepped back and felt the heel of his shoe hit something hard. He looked down without thinking and saw a flash of gold resting against his foot.

'I see you've found it,' the man said quietly.

Without thinking, Jamie reached down and grabbed the item, pulling it out of the rubble and holding it in front of him. Light flashed across the surface of the sword and danced along the hilt. The item felt strange in his hands, like a soft electric current was running through it. He was certain it was humming to him.

'Isn't she beautiful?' the man said quietly.

'She's the most amazing thing I've ever seen,' Jamie replied, without thinking.

'Whole worlds are lost in that metal. Do you know what I call her?'

Jamie shook his head, reluctant to take his eyes off the sword.

'The soul eater.'

'Why?'

'Because she eats souls, of course,' the man replied with a chuckle. 'Want to see?'

Jamie's stomach dropped. He gripped the sword hilt hard and took another step back, his feet scrabbling through the debris for purchase.

'Who are you really?' he asked, raising the sword in front of him.

'I am the moon and the stars, I am day and night. I am Wormwood, the evening star, and I have come for my prize.'

Without thinking Jamie lunged forward and stabbed towards the stranger. It was this quick movement that saved him. The sword nicked the man's shoulder, sending him tumbling backwards, a high-pitched scream bursting from his lips.

Jamie stumbled past him, sword in hand and raced for the door. Before he could reach it, the creature was upon him, its hands grabbing his shoulders and flinging him around.

'You dare to attack me with my own sword!' the creature screamed at him.

Jamie punched upwards with the sword hilt and hit the stranger square on the jaw. He fell backwards, and hit the ground with a crash.

'That was for Derek,' Jamie shouted before turning and rushing out of the door.

He raced into the dark street and began running along the road. He didn't know if the man was chasing him or not, but he wanted to put as much distance between himself and the house as quickly as he could.

He reached the street corner and slowed. A man with a dog walked past him, and a child on a bike rode lazily by. It all seemed surreal after the near-death experience he'd encountered moments before, but with an effort he slowed to a walk, and tucked the sword into the side of his leg, conscious not to draw attention to the fact he was carrying it.

Unsure what to do or where to go, Jamie's first instinct was to find a bus. If he could get out of the area, he'd be safe. He looked around for a bus stop and saw one the other side of a small playground. Without thinking he entered the park and started to make his way across. The dark enveloped him quickly, making him shudder inside. He could see the bright lights surrounding the bus stop, just the other side of the swings and he quickened his pace. Eager to get back into its warm glow.

The man stepped out from behind a slide and smiled at Jamie, his white teeth stark against the blackness that surrounded him. Jamie stopped, his heart sinking.

'Do you really think it would be that easy to take my prize from me?' the man said, his voice sounding like wind rustling through a graveyard.

'Stand back,' Jamie said, raising the sword.

The man chuckled and shook his head. 'Master Jamie,

I'm going to take your arms from your body. The pain will be exquisite. Your screams will fill the air.'

'And everyone will hear them for miles around,' Jamie replied, stepping backwards. Although he was terrified, he knew his only chance of survival was to keep the man talking. If he could just reach the exit, he'd have a chance.

'You would have thought so, my friend, but I have ways of keeping things secret. Only you and I will hear your screams.'

'What do you need this sword for anyway?'

'It is mine!' the man snarled, his nostrils flaring.

'It's much more than that, I think. No one would be this mad for a sword. You need it, don't you?' Jamie asked, taking another few steps backwards.

'You ask too many questions, little man,' the strangers said, suddenly lunging forward. Without thinking, Jamie stabbed the sword forward and it pierced the man's arm. He let out another wail of pain and jumped backwards.

'I will eat your soul for that!' he screamed.

Jamie turned and ran for the exit, all thought of defending himself gone. The man reached him before he could make more than a few strides. He felt pain rip through his shoulder as he was turned around and flung to the floor, the sword falling from his grasp.

A dark shadow, with eyes the colour of hot coals, loomed over him.

'It's time to die, little man. Remember to scream. You wouldn't want to deny me that now, would you?'

Jamie tried to scramble backwards, his heart pounding in his chest, blood seeping from his shoulder. He was a terrified animal, caught in the headlights of an oncoming car, and he was about to die. His mind screamed at him to do something, to save himself, but his body felt numb. He had no idea how to escape from the creature in front of him. Then Derek's voice popped into his terrified mind. 'What on earth are you doing, Jamie? I knew you were just as useless as the rest. You'll never be the Chairman of Abandoned Glasgow.'

Jamie ground his teeth at the sound. He hated Derek and his condescending attitude. A part of him was glad he was dead. Chairperson, you prick.

'You'll never get the rest if you kill me,' he blurted out.

The creature stopped and looked down at him. 'Are you trying to delay the inevitable, my friend? I applaud you for it, but it will do you no good. Pain is coming.

'Maybe, but you don't know if I'm telling the truth or not,' Jamie said with a confidence he didn't feel. 'I know where there are more.'

'More what?'

'Swords. I think you want more of them.'

The man grinned then winked at him. 'I will never get used to how inventive your kind are.'

'Yeah, you'd be surprised,' he said, kicking at the man's shin and bringing him tumbling to the floor. Jamie lurched to his feet and staggered away before the man could recover. He ran towards the exit with all the strength he could muster, aware that more blood had started to fall freely from his shoulder.

'You really are making this interesting, Jamie,' the man said from behind him.

Jamie didn't stop to look around, he knew it would be the death of him if he did. His focus was on the exit, just twenty yards in front of him and the inviting glow of the pavement beyond. He staggered towards it, taking in great lungsful of cold air as he did.

The man stepped casually in front of the exit, just as Jamie reached it. A wicked smile spread across his face.

'Surprise.'

Jamie staggered to a halt a few feet from him, his heart sinking. He was going to die after all.

'That was fun, now time to die, little man.' the creature said, raising the golden sword in front of him. 'What shall I start with? Your eyes I think.' He took a step forward, raising the sword above his head, then stopped. 'No, it can't be.'

Something flashed past Jamie and smashed into the man's chest, sending him hurtling backwards. Unsure what was happening, Jamie fell to the ground and instinctively covered his head.

The next few moments were filled with the sounds of fighting and cursing, then a silence that seemed to stretch out into eternity.

'You're safe now,' a quiet voice said.

Jamie looked up to the strangest sight he'd ever seen, which was saying something after his recent experiences. A man stood in front of him, his chest bare and his legs covered in fur. His feet ended in hooves and Jamie was sure that small horns jutted out of the curly hair on top of his head.

'Where is he?' Jamie asked.

'Gone. He will not stand before the Keepers of the Watch. He is not powerful enough for that yet,' the thing replied.

'He wanted the sword,' Jamie said pathetically, not sure what else to say.

'Yes, and he took it. We will get it back.'

'Who are you? I mean, thank you and all that, but who are you?'

'My name is Silas; I have been sent by a mutual friend.'

'I'll need to thank them too.'

'Yes, don't worry; you'll get your chance,' Silas replied, holding out his hand.

AND SO, IT BEGINS

Lewis shuffled his feet and groaned. He hated travelling by the fast underground car known as the chute. Even though he'd only done it once before that was enough. He ended up getting lost in the maze of tunnels below Glasgow last time, it was something he wasn't keen on repeating. His legs still felt wobbly, even though they'd arrived without incident and were now walking down a tunnel.

'Are you OK?' Charlie asked.

'I don't know. He was a real pain, but Derek didn't deserve to die that way.'

'Yeah, I know what you mean. How come we didn't know that a demon had got hold of him?'

'Derek always acted strange, how were we supposed to know?'

'Yeah, I suppose.'

'Why the hell are we going through with this?' Lewis spat. 'A guy's dead, we should be dealing with that and trying to find his killer, not messing about underground.'

'That's Bob's call,' Charlie said gently, putting her hand on his shoulder. 'We can't stop this now that the message has been sent. If we didn't show up, it would give The Dark Man an advantage. We'll mourn Derek when we've taken care of these two monsters. We'll mourn him and go looking for his killer. I can't believe that demon is your dad. I'm so sorry Lewis.'

Lewis shuddered when he thought about his dad and how he'd casually killed Derek, but he wasn't ready to talk to Charlie about his dad yet. He wasn't even ready to confront Scarlett about it, even though he had a million questions. First of which was why on earth would she fall for a demon in the first place?

'Where's that angel with the other sword? This doesn't feel right, Charlie,' he said, switching the subject.

'Don't worry, it will all go according to plan.'

Lewis looked at her sidelong and smiled. 'Yeah OK.'

Scarlett walked just behind Charlie and Lewis. She'd heard their conversation and wished she could take her son aside and tell him all about his father and explain to him that he was the one she'd gone to Edinburgh to find and kill. But now wasn't the time. Her heart had sunk when she'd heard that he'd turned up at the shop. Lewis had explained what his dad had tried to do and looked at her with accusing eyes. She'd wanted to tell him then, but Bob had insisted that they set out for the station instead. She reached out and put her hand on her son's shoulder.

'Get off,' he said, jerking away.

'Are you OK?' Charlie asked.

'Yeah, I'm fine, I just hate those bloody bullet car things, they make me feel sick,' he said, trying to change the subject.

'Really? I love them. The grains that open up the portal, the plush red seats, the speed, it's awesome.'

'Awesome,' Lewis replied, shaking his head.

'You've got to take the perks where you can,' Charlie said with a smile.

'I really don't think speeding around the sewers in a plush red coffin is a perk. I thought we were going to crash at every turn.'

'But they're magic, of course they won't crash.'

'Got that in writing, have you?'

'I don't get it. You have no problem turning into a big shaggy dog, but you don't like riding in a nice underground train.'

'Lycan, not dog, and it's not a train, it's a bloody coffin.'

'Yeah, whatever.'

'Stop your bickering you two, we're nearly there,' Bob said from the front.

Lewis saluted, and Charlie gave him the finger.

Lewis felt the now familiar sick feeling in his stomach, as they got closer to the station. It happened every time he was about to go into battle. His mind started racing, a thousand doubts hitting him all at one. What if he couldn't change? What if he wasn't strong enough? What if Charlie got hurt and he couldn't help her? What if the Dark Man didn't show up, or they weren't able to get the swords from The Gatherer? Why was he doing this instead of trying to find his demon dad? His stomach started to feel worse as his mind raced.

'We'll beat him,' Charlie said quietly beside him, a smile creeping into her eyes. Lewis simply nodded in return.

A faint light appeared in front of them, getting stronger the closer they got to it. The soft hum of a thousand voices crept into their ears, growing louder as they neared the station.

Bob stopped and turned around to face them. The bulk of their force, around fifty lycans were crouched in the tunnel, Calder amongst them, panting gently and aching from every joint. It was a crazy gamble, and one Lewis wasn't certain would work, but Bob was convinced this was the only way they could flush out The Dark Man, and his army and deal with The Gatherer at the same time.

'OK, listen up, they took the bait,' Bob said, nodding to his phone. 'That angel has just got back to me. Like we agreed back in the shop, Charlie is going to take ten men and visit The Gatherer.'

'She's taking ten people, Bob,' Fi said.

'Yeah, whatever. Ten of you go with her, Fi you choose,

and be careful with that sword, it looks sharp.'

Charlie smiled as she lifted it up in front of her face, the glow making her look menacing in the gloom.

'Lewis and me, we'll wait outside, with the rest of the crew, and say hello to The Dark Man and his troops, when they arrive. Lewis, do you have that other sword?' Lewis nodded in reply. 'Good, your job is to stick him with the pointy end; we'll work it so you can get close. He'll be expecting you to change and go at him as a lycan.'

'Are you sure this will work?' Scarlett asked.

'No, but it's the best plan we have. You and Calder go after Mono, he'll be expecting us all to go after his master.'

'I don't think Calder's well enough to face him,' Scarlett said.

'I'm fine, besides, Mono's mine,' Calder said, hefting a large axe in his hands.

'Just remember your job is to keep him busy so that Lewis can go after The Dark Man. Don't go all postal and get yourself killed in a heartbeat.'

'You're all heart, Bob,' Calder said.

'I want mine to keep beating, so do your job.'

'What about all the creatures on the concourse?' Lewis asked.

'Like I said, they'll all scarper when the fighting begins.'

'I hope you're right.'

'I'm right, trust me,' Bob replied with a wide grin. 'OK, everyone know what they're about? Fi, have you chosen your crew?'

'Yep, but we're not happy about this, Bob, you should have told us about The Dark Man earlier.' The lycans next to her mumbled their agreement.

'Whatever, we don't have time for this, let's go.'

They made their way towards the entrance, the light growing alongside the sounds of talking. Lewis felt his stomach lurch once again and took in a deep breath. The smell of damp and earth filling his nostrils, the sharp tang of magic tickling the back of his throat. His palms started to sweat at the thought of the oncoming battle, and his body itched to change, but somehow he managed to keep the magic inside him.

'How did Bob get a signal down here?' Charlie mused.

'Magic,' Lewis replied.

'Will we ever get used to this, do you think?' Charlie whispered beside him.

'Used to what?'

'All of this, the magic, changing into a big dog, the power, the fact that there are demons walking the earth, all of it.'

'Now's not the time for a philosophical chat, Charlie, and we're lycans, not dogs.'

'Come on, you must wonder about it all?'

'Honestly, I haven't had the time to consider what I'm having for dinner, let alone why I can turn into a big dog.'

'Lycan.'

'Whatever.'

'But why us? Why are we royalty and not someone else?'

'Accident of birth, you me and Prince William, although I'm certain he can't turn into a lycan.'

'Maybe a werewolf, though?' Charlie said with a grin.

Lewis laughed and shook his head. It was a strange conversation to have before a battle, but at least the urge to change had settled down. The thought of his dad still lingered in the back of his mind, however; he wondered if the link with a demon really did make him a Prince of the Blood. They entered the cavernous platform and it struck Lewis for the first time that the ceiling disappeared into the gloom. There was no concrete or brick ceiling like there would have been in a normal station, and the platform itself was the width of a football pitch. Not really like a normal platform at all.

Maybe it's magic? he thought to himself. It wouldn't be the first time in this crazy adventure that things seemed strange.

The platform was full of magical creatures, just like on their previous visits. Most were clustered in groups, talking in hushed voices that created the soft hum they'd heard in the tunnel. One or two were sitting on the ground, if indeed a tree can ever really sit on the ground. A group of what looked like green goblins were sitting together playing cards.

Charlie gave his arm a quick squeeze, then set of to visit The Gatherer. Lewis moved closer to the remaining lycans, still unsure of what to do next. Bob took them through the crowd, gently pushing creatures out of his way as he did.

'The Prince of the Blood,' a water nymph said and the hum around them immediately stopped. The creature flowed towards him and then, to Lewis's amazement, went down on one knee and bowed its head. Suddenly creatures around him all began to bend the knee. Before long a sea of bowed heads stretched out before him. Unsure what to do, Lewis simply stood and stared.

'The Prince of the Blood thanks you for your loyalty and pledges fealty to the cause. We are one,' Bob said from behind him.

'We are one,' the bowed heads intoned in union, before the creatures all rose and resumed what they were doing.

'What the hell was that?' Lewis asked.

'An act of loyalty. An important one, seeing as what's coming,' Bob replied.

'That didn't happen last time. Who is one?'

'You managed to keep your head down the last time. We are all one. I'm not really sure what it means; Blaine should have told you. I think it means we're all in it together. Magical creatures united and all that.'

'It means we come from the one source,' Calder interjected.

'What source?'

'I think you've seen it, the tree?'

'Oh, yeah, the tree that grows in the cave. That's weird, which is saying something in this place.'

'We're nothing without it.'

'Speak for yourself,' Bob said. 'Come on, let's get over to the far side. If he comes, it will probably be through the same tunnels we did. Let's put a lot of magical creatures between us, before he arrives.' They made their way through the crowd, the odd creature tipping its forelock at Lewis, still more eyeing him suspiciously.

'I bet that gets boring really quickly?' Calder laughed.

'You have no idea.'

Before long, they reached the edge of the platform and turned around to face the crowd.

'What now?' Midgy asked.

'Hello, I didn't know you were here. Shouldn't you be with Charlie?'

'Nope, we're not joined at the hip or anything.'

'We wait. Anyone fancy a game of cards?' Bob replied. The crew shuffled their feet and avoided eye contact with him; most had been on the wrong end of a card thrashing and one or two still owed him money. 'Suit yourself.'

After a few minutes of standing, Lewis sat down on the cold platform. It made him a little less conspicuous and stopped some of the creatures coming over to tip their forelock, or worse grab his knee as one or two had done.

'Bob,' a voice whispered from the crowd.

'Beth,' Bob hissed, rushing over to a small girl, who had appeared from the throng. He took her in his arms and marched her back to the lycans. 'What are you doing here on your own? They're going to be here any second, you'll blow everything if they see you.'

'I had to get away, I think they suspect me,' the girl replied.

'Who's this?' Lewis asked.

'Never mind.'

'I'm Beth, are you him?' the girl asked, freeing herself from Bob's grip and coming over.

'Yes, I'm him.'

'I thought you'd be taller.'

'They all say that.'

The girl smiled at him manically, tilting her head and stepping back, as if to get a better look. 'He commands, and I obey,' she said, reaching inside her overcoat and pulling out a sword. At first Lewis thought she was going to hand it to him, but she screamed at the top of her lungs and lunged towards him, the sword held high above her head. He changed without thinking, jumping back on his newly created hind legs. The sword missed his torso by inches, but it took a gouge out of his thigh. He let out a roar of pain and tumbled to the ground, then all hell broke loose.

Bob screamed, lycans turned, magical creatures fled and Beth lunged, bringing the sword down in a vicious swing that would have separated Lewis's head from his body, if he hadn't rolled away at the last moment. She screamed, this time in frustration and brought the sword down repeatedly, trying to connect with any part of him. Each time he managed to roll away, then he gained his footing, as Beth overreached and stumbled to the floor. Raising to his full height he growled and prepared to lunge at his attacker.

'Stop! She doesn't know what she's doing,' Bob shouted, racing in between the two foes.

Lewis stopped and growled at Bob. 'She's one of us, they've hypnotised her or something, she's working for us,' Bob said.

Lewis turned back into a human and stepped away, panting. 'What the hell?' he gasped.

'I sent two of them into the zoo, Beth was my second ace in the hole. Beth,' he said turning towards her, 'it's OK, you're safe. They can't hurt you now, put the sword down.'

'Where did they get that sword, Bob,' Scarlett asked.

'Looks like the one Jillian took; where the hell is she?'

'Looks like there's more than one traitor,' Scarlett said through gritted teeth.

'Beth, it's me, put the sword down, you don't need to do this.'

Beth staggered back, staring between Lewis, Scarlett and Bob, then dropped the sword and put her head in her hands.

'They made me do it, they made me want to kill him,' she sobbed.

'It's OK, we're all here,' Bob said soothingly, putting his arm around her trembling shoulders.

'So, the traitor reveals herself,' Mono said, appearing

from the crowd. 'We had our suspicions, but here it is. You'll stop at nothing to cause chaos, Bob.'

'You!' Bob growled.

'I should have known she was one of you, she can't even follow a simple instruction; definitely a lycan.'

'You're a dead man,' Calder said, pushing forward, his face Scarlett, staring daggers at Mono.

'I'm already dead, you silly little man, just like your family.'

Calder screamed and rushed at Mono, the axe held in his grip. The creature waited until he came close, then simply side stepped out of his way.

Werewolves suddenly appeared from the crowd and began to surround the lycans.

'Change!' Guils shouted. Lewis began to phase then stopped himself, remembering at the last second that he was supposed to face The Dark Man as a human. He pushed past a sea of furry bodies, instead and grabbed the sword that lay forgotten on the ground. Hefting it in his right hand, he drew the second one with his left and dived into the fight.

A DIAMOND IN THE
ROUGH

C harlie took a deep breath and entered the cave. Paying the dirty little man holding the black book a gold coin to enter the cavern was still strange to her, but not as strange as the two headed dog that lay across the entrance, and only got out of the way when the payment was made. She'd seen many strange things since becoming a lycan but that was definitely one of the weirdest. The heat hit her as soon as she entered the cavern, a cloying warmth that clung to her like wet clothes. The stench came next, a mixture of rotting eggs, putrid meat and sour milk. She tried not to gag but couldn't help herself. The crew around her groaned in unison. Fi covered her mouth, 'My God that's awful,' she said.

'It is the smell of truth,' a voice said from the centre of the room. As before, The Gatherer sat cross legged in a small clearing at the centre of the cave. His greasy hair hung in strands across his face, while his blackened hands played with a frayed piece of string.

'The Princess of the Blood has graced us with her

presence, but I fear she does not have grace in her heart.'

'You have two swords, we need them,' Charlie said, through her fingers.

'Subtle,' Fi whispered.

'I wondered when you would come for me. They are not yours, my princess. They belong to me, one a fair bargain, the other my possession all along.'

'So you do have your own sword?'

'This is no secret, I am a demon, as you say.'

'It's keeping you here, demon; it's time to go back to where you came from, you and the rest of your hell hoard.'

'You do not know what I do, you have no idea what I keep together. Attack me and you attack yourself.

'We need those swords, it's that simple.'

'Then come and take them.'

Charlie turned and felt the rest of the crew phase around her. She prepared to lunge towards the seated monster, when suddenly the world went dark. She fell to her knees as a cold draft washed over her, sending shivers down her spine. The world had become a pitch-black hole; no spot of light could be seen wherever Charlie looked.

'What the hell,' Fi said beside her.

'Fi, are you alright?'

'It's all gone black.'

'Stay where you are, it's him, he's done something to our eye sight.'

With an effort Charlie closed her eyes and opened up her ears and nostrils. The putrid smell of the cave was still there, and she could hear someone walking towards her.

'What good are you without your eyes?' The Gatherer asked. 'But what would happen if you lost your other senses too?'

Charlie felt the world tilt on its axis and she began flailing around, despite the fact that moments before she'd knelt on solid ground. She felt herself suddenly falling through the blackness, her arms and legs flapping uselessly at her sides. The wind rushed in her ears and raced through her hair. Her eyes began to stream despite the darkness and her ears popped. Her mind screamed at her that this wasn't real, but the rushing wind and the feeling of helpless falling told her otherwise. After what seemed an age, a point of light appeared on the horizon. It grew quickly and engulfed her. Flashes of green, red, brown and yellow raced across her vision, until she suddenly felt solid ground beneath her feet and came to a juddering stop. The wind was knocked out of her as she connected with the ground and she lay there for several moments, unsure if anything was broken. With an effort she pulled her legs underneath herself and pushed up into a standing position. A wave of nausea raced through her. When the feeling eventually subsided, she opened her eyes to a glorious vista. A large valley was laid out before her, covered in green grass and squares of golden wheat. A small cottage was nestled at the bottom, a lazy curl of smoke rising from its chimney.

The air was filled with birdsong, while a single white cloud slid across a bright blue sky. Charlie could feel the sun warm her face and a soft breeze tickle her ears.

'This isn't real,' she said out loud, to no one in particular, the twittering of birds her only response.

She turned around to see an identical view spread out behind her, a twin cottage nestled into the bottom of that valley too. Either she was in some alternate reality, or The Gatherer was playing with her mind. The thought that she was actually still in the cave, with the monster able to do anything to her while he sent her mind somewhere else, made her feel sick. She had to get out of his grip but had no idea how to do that. She decided to make her way down the valley towards the cottage, hoping that the walk would give her inspiration.

Half way down, she heard a scream emanate from behind a hedge in front of her. Charlie stumbled backwards and began to phase as she fell to the ground. To her horror nothing happened. The well she went to simply wasn't there, the power normally buzzing through her, was silent. She looked up to see Fi rushing towards her.

'Fi!' she screamed, 'it's me.' Fi scrambled to a stop just

in front of her, her eyes as wide as saucers, her chest heaving as she panted for breath.

'Charlie,' she gasped, before falling to the ground in front of her. 'Thank God it's you. You looked like The Dark Man when you walked down the hill. I didn't know what to do, you were coming towards me, and I couldn't hide. I can't change Charlie, I have no power. I was going to try and rip your head off instead.'

'I can't change either, I think it's The Gatherer, he's playing with our minds. I don't think we're really here, if that makes sense?'

'I guess, but how the hell can he do that to all of us, and where are the others?'

'No idea, but we need to get this sorted as soon as we can, I dread to think what he's doing while our minds are locked like this.'

'I never thought of that. Thanks for making things worse.'

'I was going down to that cottage to see if there are any answers there.' Fi nodded and helped Charlie up off the floor.

'It's as good a plan as any, I guess.'

They made their way down into the valley floor without further incident and were soon standing in front of the cottage door. It was a picture out of a country scene. A perfect little cottage with a thatched roof and a bright red front door. Roses grew out front, while ivy clung to the side wall.

'Lovely,' Fi said.

'Yeah, so was the one Hansel and Gretel found,' Charlie replied, sure they were going to find a witch waiting inside.

'It has that feel about it.'

Charlie turned inward once again, trying to channel her power, but there was still nothing there. They were going to have to do this old school.

'What if he's in there, or some other demon?' Fi asked.

'If he is, then we'll deal with him.'

'Without our powers?'

'Yes, without our powers.'

'You can go first,' Fi said, gently pushing Charlie towards the door.

'It's probably locked anyway.' She reached out and depressed the latch. It clicked loudly and the door began to swing inwards as she pushed. Charlie gagged as the smell of rotting garbage hit her.

'I guess we're still in the cave,' Fi said, covering her mouth.

Grimacing, Charlie pressed forward into the darkness, hoping that her eyes had time to adjust before she was attacked. Candles flared as she stepped over the threshold, revealing a cosy sitting room containing a chunky armchair and a roaring fire. Towards the back she could see a door that led to a kitchen beyond.

'Looks OK,' she said before walking further into the room.

Despite the idyllic scene something felt off. The room seemed to close in on them the further they went in, the bright white walls leaning forward to reach out for them. Charlie shuffled around the furniture and made her way towards the kitchen, panic starting to bubble in her stomach. She was certain the walls would close in on her if she remained in the living room much longer. The stench of rotting food had grown stronger the closer she got to the kitchen door, and she was certain she could see a body lying flat on the floor. She entered the room feeling relieved that the walls had stayed where they were, but it was short lived; the body on the floor was Lewis. She lurched towards him, a cry rising in her throat.

'Stop!' Fi said, grabbing her by the arm and pulling her backwards. 'It's not him, it's in your mind.' Charlie pulled against her, desperate to reach the body. If she could have changed and bitten Fi's arm off, she would have.

'Think about it!' Fi hissed next to her, 'how the hell could he be here in your head?'

'You are.'

'Probably because you're in my head. He's outside on

the concourse, waiting for The Dark Man and trying to give you time to get the swords. This is that smelly guy's doing, don't fall for his crap.'

Charlie eased back as she contemplated what Fi had said. There was no way that Lewis would be here, a part of her knew that, but he looked so real lying there.'

'OK,' she said eventually, 'let's leave him there.'

'Good choice, my love, it's not him and you know it.' Charlie whirled around at the sound of the voice, then staggered back into the kitchen table. Her gran was standing at the kitchen door that led to the garden, a basket of flowers in her arms.

'Gran,' Charlie gasped.

'Yes and no. He can't see me here, but you can. Hello Fi.'

'Hello, Doris, nice to see you again, we've missed you,' she said, smiling and shaking her head

'I've missed you all, too, especially you, my dear,' she said walking towards Charlie and taking her in her arms.

Charlie held back at first, then the soft smell of lavender hit her and she knew this was her Gran. She hugged her back, fiercely. Without realising she began to sob into her Gran's shoulder, great hacking cries that started in her stomach.

'That's it, get it all out. I know it's been hard. I'm so sorry for not being there for you.'

'Why did you leave me?' Charlie asked, when she was finally able to get out a question.

'Oh, Charlie. It was my fault for leaving you with Blaine, I know that now, but I would never have left you unless I thought you were safe. It was too late when I realised you were in danger, they took me away from you.'

'You're really gone, aren't you?'

'Yes, but a part of me will always live in your heart. We're family. We have a bond even death can't break. I'll always watch over you.'

'How can we see you now?' Fi asked.

'No idea. I assume it's something to do with The

Gatherer, and the magic he's using. He shouldn't be able to control your minds like this, either, it's power way beyond his capabilities. At least I thought it was. Charlie, you have to go back to the cave and kill him. He's far more dangerous than we thought. If he's conquered mind control, God knows what he will do next.'

'I'd love to get out of here, but I can't. Neither of us can feel our magic. He's taken it away.'

Doris screwed her face up thoughtfully, pulled out a chair and sat down. 'Sit down both of you, but mind that body.' They both joined her at the table, Charlie at the opposite side to the body lying on the floor.

'He can't take your magic away from you, no one can except God, and I'm not really sure she can either. He's taken away the thought of it, that's all. Look deep inside yourself, as deep as you can. Search the very essence of your power. It will be there, I promise.'

Charlie nodded and closed her eyes. It was hard to concentrate at first, she wanted to hold her Gran's hand and stay here with her forever. She took a deep breath and let her mind wander. An image of the body on the floor came to mind and she shuddered, then an image of a giant picking her up, then the golden sword, light flashing off the blade. Finally, she settled on the image of a picnic, perhaps one of her happiest thoughts. The sun was high in the sky, birds twittered in the distance. A gentle breeze rustled through the grass and the sound of laughter wafted on the air. A large blanket was spread out in front of her filled with plates of sandwiches, sausage rolls, crisps and pop. A large Victoria sponge sat proudly in the centre.

'Where shall we start?' her Gran asked from across the blanket. 'There are so many delicious things.'

'Sausage roll,' Charlie replied.

'They were always your favourite, OK, get stuck in.'

Charlie reached across and grabbed two sausage rolls, stuffing one in her mouth. The taste of buttery pastry filled her mouth and she groaned in pleasure.

'Take your time,' her Gran said laughing, 'we've got all

day.'

Charlie stopped chewing and looked up at her. 'We don't, though, do we? I need to get out of here.'

'Yes,' her Gran replied, nodding, 'you can leave anytime you want, it's all down to you.'

'I've been trying.'

'No, you've been reminiscing because it's easier. Put the food down and concentrate.'

'On what? I've been trying.'

'It doesn't have to be hard. Just look inside as I said. Your power is there.'

Charlie closed her eyes and sighed. She looked inwards this time, imagining her power as a great globe of light sitting in the pit of her stomach. She watched as it swelled and grew, changing colour from silver, to red, to gold.

'That's it, you're doing it,' she heard her Gran say. 'You too, Fi, concentrate on your power. Keep going, Charlie, and remember I love you.'

The globe of light continued to grow. She felt it swell inside her, filling her with warmth. Her veins started to sizzle and her muscles stretch. Her bones began to crack and the now familiar pain of changing took over. A muffled cry turned into an angry growl then a ferocious roar. A pinpoint of white light appeared in front of Charlie. It quickly grew into a large disc, then expanded into a hole the size of a werewolf. She leaped forward towards the light and was instantly back inside her own body, inside the cave. Without thinking, she grabbed the hilt of the sword at her side, and brought it up in front of her face. It made contact with The Gatherer's sword, the sound ringing out across the cavern, bouncing off the walls and dislodging loose stones and dirt.

'Sneaky,' Charlie said, raising off the floor and preparing to fight.

THE BATTLE OF THREE ARMIES

Despite Bob's confidence that they would scarper at the first sign of trouble, most of the magical creatures stayed on the platform as the Werewolves fought the lycans. Many were incensed that they would bring violence to such a magical place and quickly formed into their own gangs, attacking werewolves and lycans alike.

Lewis stood at the centre of the chaos, desperate to help out but knowing that he couldn't change if he was ever going to face The Dark Man and kill him. He'd managed to kill one werewolf with a sword but the rest had steered clear of him. Beth stood next to him, a confused look on her face. A lycan raced past, the arm of a werewolf hanging from its mouth.

'Aren't you going to help out?' Lewis asked.

'What?' Beth replied, looking at him stupidly.

'You're a lycan, and we need your help. Get changed and get stuck in.'

'What about you?'

'I can't, I'm waiting for someone.'

'I don't know who's on which side, I've never been in a

fight before,' Beth said, sidestepping a werewolf, as it rolled past.

'Look, I don't know what you did before but you're a lycan and we need your help. The ones with the red eyes are werewolves, you attack them, got it?'

Beth stood looking at him for a moment, then nodded. 'OK,' she said, stepping back. Lewis watched as she changed then hurled herself into the mass of fighting bodies in front of them.

'Be careful,' Lewis shouted after her for no reason in particular. He hefted the swords in his hands, still feeling useless as he watched his fellow lycans fight and die in front of him.

'You done wrong, Prince, you brought fighting to this place, you done wrong!' a green skinned creature said, as it appeared in front of him.

'Gral,' Lewis said, remembering him from their last visit to the station. 'The werewolves are attacking us, we don't want to fight them, we only want to defeat The Dark Man.'

'You brought an army, you want to fight. Fight me!' the creature screamed before lunging at Lewis.

Without thinking, Lewis brought one of the swords up and across in a wide arc, aiming to sever the creature's head from its body. At the last minute Gral raised his arm, and the sword bounced off one of the metal bands he wore on his wrists, sending bright sparks fizzing into the air. Without a pause, the creature stepped inside Lewis's defences and punched him squarely in the jaw. Lewis staggered back and fell to the floor, one of the swords falling from his hand and rattling across the concrete. Without thinking, Lewis changed, and jumped up off the floor. With a growl he dived at Gral, the impact sending them both backwards and into the mass of fighting bodies. Gral grabbed and held him in a desperate embrace, squeezing harder and harder. Lewis bit, clawed and snarled as he rolled across the floor. He could feel his bones start to creak as the pressure grew, and he writhed and squirmed, trying to find a way to escape, or at least bite Gral's head off. The creature huffed and puffed with the effort of holding Lewis in a tight embrace, his muscles bulging and his eyes popping out of this head. The world started to fade and blue stars began to dance across Lewis's vision. He could feel the power seeping from his bones and wondered if Gral would inherit it, if he defeated him. The pressure suddenly stopped just as Lewis reached the edge of consciousness and he rolled out of the creature's deadly embrace and lay on the floor panting for breath. He knew he should move and defend himself, but his arms and legs refused to obey. He lay instead like a wounded fish, his mouth opening and closing with each ragged breath he took. After what seemed like an age, during which time he was sure a werewolf would come across and take his head, he felt the power return to his limbs, and he staggered up off the floor. The battle still raged on around him, but another creature had entered the fray. The Dark Man stood a few feet away, the two swords Lewis had dropped held in each of his hands. Blue blood dripped from one, creating a small pool at the demon's feet.

'We meet again,' Lewis heard the creature say inside his head, a cruel smile spread across his face. 'I was going to kill you while you lay there helpless but where is the fun in that? You sent me back to Hell, and you need to pay for that insult. A quick death would be too easy.'

'You were sent back to where you belong. You should not be in this realm,' Lewis responded in his mind.

'So you say, but I am a creature of the night, a prince of the dark and I do not answer to you.'

'You will do, demon.'

Lewis drew himself up to his full height. The Dark Man had both swords, there was no way he could beat him in his human form, and figured this was his only chance. He knew Bob would be shaking his head if he could see, but you had to make lemonade when all you had was lemons. A deep growl emanated from him as he readied himself for the charge. He leaned back onto his powerful hind legs and launched himself forward, praying he had enough speed and strength to get inside The Dark Man's defences.

Calder was literally in the dark. It enveloped him like a thick black shroud. He could almost feel it pressing down, its weight trying to push him into the filthy earth at his feet. It had all started so well. He'd attacked Mono with a recklessness that should have got him killed instantly, but the creature had been unprepared for the ferocity of the attack. Calder had channelled all his anger and hate, all his pain and suffering into his onslaught. He wanted to rip the creature's head from its shoulders and wear his ridiculously bright purple tie as a trophy. He could see his family in his mind's eye, urging him on, telling him to kill the monster in front of him. But things hadn't gone to plan. Rather than facing him, Mono had run. Calder had watched, stunned, as the creature dived from the platform and ran down the empty track. Then he realised Mono was getting away and raced after him. He jumped in between the old tracks and stumbled over the sleepers. Why they were still there when the station had been abandoned decades before he didn't know, but he had no time to ponder, Mono was already getting further away from him. Despite his injuries, he quickened his pace, determined to catch him as quickly as he could and make him pay. He was enveloped by the tunnel as it curved away from the station, the sounds of fighting quickly fading into memory. A thin line of blue lights on the tunnel roof helped him keep up a steady pace, and he began gaining on his prey. He could see the back of Mono's suit rising and falling in front of him, as the monster ran down the middle of the track, then he stumbled and fell. Calder quickened his pace again, in anticipation of catching him, but the creature jumped up quickly and turned to his left, disappearing down a dark side tunnel. Calder followed, the blackness sucking him in, and forcing him to slow his pace to a walk. He knew the monster could be just in front of him, but he dared not race forward. Mono wasn't human and could probably see in the dark. Calder reached out to his right and felt for the tunnel wall. His fingers made contact with its damp surface, and he used it as a guide to help him down the tunnel. The uneven floor meant he stumbled along, despite the wall's steady presence, and he fell to his knees several times. He nearly broke his ankle as he stepped into a hole. He was sure that Mono was well down the tunnel by now, and racing away to freedom, but he carried on anyway, not willing to admit to himself, or his family, that he had failed them again.

'They begged for mercy before I killed them,' Mono's blank voice said from the darkness in front of Calder. 'They were willing to give you up, did you know that? They were willing to tell me anything I wanted, to give away your darkest secrets, if only I would let them live. What's it like to know that your own family was willing to betray you?'

'Liar!' Calder screamed into the darkness. Mono's cold chuckles floated past him in response.

'There was no loyalty in your family Calder, but then again, what can you expect from those whose blood has little magic? You are weak Calder, and your family were weaker.'

'Your master is the prince of lies, I don't believe a word that comes out of your mouth,' Calder spat back.

'Yes, you do, I can hear it in your rage.'

'Come out and face me you coward. I'm just a weakling with hardly any magic, it should be easy to kill me.'

'And miss the opportunity to torment you a little, I don't think so, besides I have a message for you. It was the last thing your wife said before she died, would you like to hear it?'

Calder stopped in his tracks and gritted his teeth. He knew the creature was lying, but he had to hear him out.

'What did she say?' he choked.

'She said to tell you she loved you, despite all the disappointments. That she tried hard to forgive you your failure, that she never liked your father, and your daughter isn't yours. Apparently, she had an affair with a werewolf to make sure that one of her children had a decent amount of magical power in their blood. You just can't trust people these days.'

'I can't trust you,' Calder replied, following the sound of Mono's voice as he made his way steadily down the tunnel.

'Of course you can't trust me, but that's not the problem. You can't be sure how much is true and how much is lies, that's the problem. Am I making it up, or did she really say those things?'

'It doesn't matter, you're going to die either way.'

'Come and get me, then,' Mono said, two bright spots of light suddenly appearing in front of Calder. He stepped back from the blinding lights, but it was too late to avoid Mono's crushing blow. It hit him on the side of the head and sent him reeling to the ground. The world had turned on its axis once again. Up was down, and down was up. Calder knew he was in mortal danger, but he couldn't stop the blue fairies that raced across his vision or the feeling that he was suddenly in a faraway place, looking down on his prone body. He watched as Mono came into view, illuminated by the strange light that emanated from his eyes. He could do nothing as the creature loomed over him, a strange smile creasing his face. Mono spoke to him, but the sound seemed to be coming from far away, like the monster was speaking down a long tube.

'Can't hear you,' Calder mumbled.

Mono shook his head and grabbed him by the shoulder, lifting him up off the ground and holding him up in front of him.

'Can you hear me now?'

Calder lifted his head off his shoulders and blinked an acknowledgement.

'You're going to die now, but it won't be pleasant or quick. You caused my master untold misery when you helped send him back to hell, and you need to pay for that.'

Calder looked straight into Mono's bright eyes and smiled. He knew he was about to die but he was going to take this creature with him, if he could. With an effort, he reached down and put his hand inside his jacket pocket.

'Did I really cause him misery?'

'You have no idea.'

'Good, he's a demon and deserves it.' Calder brought the screwdriver out of his pocket and pushed it up into the underside of Mono's chin with all his might. The creature gave a low moan, dropped Calder to the ground and staggered backwards. Reaching up he grabbed the screwdriver's handle and began to pull, but Calder's aim had been true. The screwdriver's tip had pierced through Mono's tongue, and lodged itself between two of his top teeth. Black blood began to seep over the handle and soak Mono's hand. His head dipped downwards with every pull on the handle, and every pull was accompanied by a low moan.

'That's for my wife, you bastard,' Calder said quietly. He stood up and stepped towards the struggling creature and punched the screwdriver upwards with all his might. The blow pushed it through Mono's palate and into his left eyeball, popping it as the tip burst through, and turning off one of the lights. Mono groaned once more and staggered further back into the gloom.

'That is for my kids.'

Calder chased after the single beam of light that was left, eager to finish him off. He saw him desperately trying to dislodge the screwdriver and rushed forward, preparing the killing blow. He didn't see the hand until it was wrapped around his neck. Mono's vice like grip squeezed the breath from Calder's throat. He lifted him off his feet and with an effort squeezed as hard as he could. Calder gave a single wheeze then his neck broke with a loud crack. Mono dropped him to the floor and staggered backwards, the pain and disorientation from the loss of blood making him dizzy. He took one unsteady step forward then another. A smile split his pierced face and he chuckled despite the pain. If he'd been able to, he would have gloated over Calder's dead body. He stepped around the corpse and staggered another few steps forward. Red mist began to form in front of his eye, and the world became smaller. A part of Mono knew he was about to pass out, but he continued on down the tunnel. He stepped into a hole on his next stride and it sent him tumbling forward like a felled tree. He hit the ground with a thud, the screwdriver punching upwards and into his brain. The light in Mono's remaining eye blinked and went out, but the smile remained on his ruined face.

Scarlett was furious. The angel who they thought had been on their side had attacked her twice since the fighting had begun. She'd nearly cornered her, only to be thwarted by an angry water nymph. It had smashed into her just as she was about to bite the angel's head off. Now she lay in a watery heap on the platform floor, as chaos ensued around her. She lifted her head, trying to see where the traitor had gone, but saw no sign of her. Scarlett got to her feet and dived into the fray. If she couldn't find the angel, she was going to kill a few werewolves instead. The red mist descended as she fought werewolf after werewolf, with the odd magical creature appearing in front of her for good measure. Bob had been confident that they would all disappear as soon as the fighting started, but neither of them had counted on their anger and ferocity, and it pained her as she crushed a goblin beneath her massive paws. She tried to stick to attacking werewolves, but it was impossible to avoid other creatures in the heat of battle.

After dodging a few creatures and wrestling with a particularly large werewolf, she staggered into a circle of space and stopped to look around. Writhing bodies surrounded her, but none wore the white coat of the angel. Grimly she dived back into the chaos, knocking a centaur unconscious and biting the shoulder of a jet-black wolf. Suddenly she came up against the platform wall and stopped once again to look around. Jillian Lightfoot was leaning against the wall a few dozen paces away, clearly trying to disappear into the concrete. Scarlett growled and dived towards her. A blast hit her just as she was about to dive on top of her foe. It sent her crashing into the wall before sliding down into a heap on the platform floor. Dazed, she looked up into the angel's cold eyes.

'Does it hurt? Good; it will be nothing more than a splinter compared to the pain you have caused me. I would have come for your family long ago, if there had been an opportunity but I am a patient creature and revenge is a dish best served cold, as they say.'

'What are you talking about? Why have you betrayed us?' a changed Scarlett asked groggily.

'Trust you not to know your own family's past, I expected nothing less. Your family has caused pain and chaos throughout the ages, but it ends here and now.'

Scarlett had no idea what the angel was talking about and needed a few minutes to clear her head, so she simply shrugged and stared back at her foe.

'I'm sure you would do anything to save your family. I was no different,' the angel said, crouching down and leaning in. 'We are forbidden to marry or have children, it's God's law, did you know that? Of course you didn't. Like most of God's laws, it's there to be broken. I broke it in the most complete way. I fell in love with a mortal. Long ago, when I was new to this world of men, I met the love of my life. I loved her so deeply, that I was willing to give up my life in the heavenly host, to make myself mortal and live out my days in love and peace. Stupidly, I thought I could hide this from God, but that could never happen. She sent your ancestor to remind me of the law. He did it in the most brutal way possible. He claimed my love was a witch and hanged her in the Gallowgate. I cannot explain to you the depths of the pain I felt. God exiled me to heaven, for my own good, and I have watched on in pain and fury ever since, biding my time until I was allowed back down onto earth once again. I could not take my revenge on the man who condemned my love, but I can on his ancestors. This is the greatest irony of all. He claimed my lover was a witch when she was nothing but a mortal woman, all the time hiding the fact that he was the head of a family of lycans. It took all of my strength not to reach out and start ripping heads from shoulders the first time I saw you and your son in the shop. I sent the minotaur into the basement of that museum, hoping that he would give me some relief by ridding me of your troublesome son, but he got away and a mortal man died in his stead. Your family has been lucky at every turn, but it ends tonight. The Dark Man and his army will crush your pathetic little band of lycans, and I will rejoice in your failure. Before then, I will take you from this earth and your son will know who killed you before The Dark Man takes his head.'

'You're an angel, you're pure love,' Scarlett said.

'My love died at the end of a hangman's noose; since then I have had nothing but hate and loathing for your kind.'

'God will know this. She will seek you out.'

'She's far too busy to worry about her trusted angel, besides, how do you know she didn't authorise this?'

'Why would she?'

'Because you are all an abomination, you flout her laws with your magic and royal blood. I warned you all that she wanted an end to this, but you didn't listen. Here's the rub of it, she didn't just want an end to the fighting she wants an end to you all. God's plan is to remove you from this world. Tell me, what do you think about that?'

'You're a liar.'

'We'll see.' Jillian reached down and hauled Scarlett up from the floor and pushed her against the concrete wall. 'It's time to say goodbye, lycan. Say hello to your ancestor when you greet him in hell.'

Scarlett felt pressure grow across her body as the angel used her powers to push her against the wall. She tried to change but the pressure grew quickly and became so great she couldn't concentrate on channelling her power. Her head felt like it was about to explode, her lungs began to compress and her back screamed as her bones grated against the wall. She began to lose consciousness and briefly wondered if her son would miss her, when the pressure abruptly ceased and she fell to the ground, gasping for breath. She looked up to see Bob, in lycan form, standing over her, growling at the angel.

'It doesn't matter which one of you dies first, Bob, you're all going to hell.' Bob growled in response and dived at Lightfoot. She lifted her hands and tried to push him back with her powers, but he was too quick and hit her squarely in the chest, throwing her backwards into a group of writhing werewolves and lycans.

Bob reached down and picked Scarlett up off the floor using his massive paws.

'It's OK, I'm fine,' she reassured him. 'We'd better get back to it before she finishes off those fighters.' Bob grunted in response and, despite the pain in her head and back, Scarlett changed and dived back into the fight.

Lewis was bleeding from myriad cuts caused by the swords that The Dark Man wielded. He'd tried desperately to avoid the sharp blades, had changed back into his human form and reached out countless times with his powers, trying to crush The Dark Man's black heart, as he had done before. The creature was too quick for him, and the flashing swords were a dangerous distraction. Besides, that would only send him back to hell like last time. He needed to kill him and that meant getting the swords. The only way he was going to do that was in his human form.

'You look like you're tiring.' The Dark Man taunted him.

'I'm strong enough for you.'

'Not in your human form. I will not make the same mistake as last time. You will not pull me in with your powers.'

'We'll see,' Lewis replied before darting forward and falling to his knees at the last minute, hoping to bowl the creature over. The Dark Man had anticipated the move and jumped backwards at the crucial moment, bringing one of the swords down and across Lewis's back before he could dive out of the way. Pain lashed across his back, and he felt warm blood start seep under his shirt.

'You are weaker with each cut. How much longer do you think you can continue? By the way, I must thank you for getting rid of Blaine. He was guarding a portal in that shop of his, I'm sure you knew that. With him gone, it will be far easier to bring my brothers through. What fun we will have in this world now that the keep of the gate has gone. He'd kept that portal closed for millennia, I bet you didn't know that.'

The Dark Man lunged forward again, birling both

swords in front of him. Lewis stumbled backwards and crashed into a lycan who was finishing off a werewolf. They both fell to the ground in a heap, the lycan falling on top of him. The Dark Man was on them in an instant and plunged one of the swords into the lycan's back. The creature moaned in pain then slumped over Lewis, his body instantly becoming a dead weight. He felt the body tremble and writhe on top of him as it changed back into a human. The dead man's head rested on Lewis's shoulder, his eyes, mere inches away, staring at him blankly.

'I'm almost sorry to disturb you, but we have business to finish,' The Dark Man said from above.

Lewis saw the creature's boots appear at either side of his head and looked up to see a sword point hanging over him. Instinct took over and he changed instantly, the strength rushing through him, as his hands turned to paws and his mouth turned into a snarling maw. He pushed the dead man up and off himself, the body banging into The Dark Man's legs and sending him to the ground. Lewis jumped onto his hind legs and turned toward the creature, but The Dark Man was already back onto his feet, but he only held one sword in his hands this time.

'I keep underestimating you, but no more. Come at me, lycan, and I will pierce your heart with this sword.'

Lewis bared his teeth and growled. He dived forward, determined to rip the creature's head from his shoulders, his paws extended, claws outstretched and sharp. The Dark Man dived to his left at the last moment, missing Lewis's snapping teeth by inches. Lewis scrambled across the now empty ground and came to a stop in front of a dying werewolf. He barely had time to register him before The Dark Man came rushing forward, the sword held high above his head. Lewis jumped forward hoping to get under the sword's arc, and take the monster's legs from him once again, but the demon anticipated this move too and came to a shuddering stop, before lashing out with his right foot and hitting Lewis square in the jaw. Stars flashed across his vision as he fell to the ground in a heap. A part of him knew he had seconds before the sword detached his head from his shoulders, but the world was spinning and his head felt like it was about to explode. He tried to get his limbs to move, but all he could managed was to tremble on the ground. It seemed like lying on the ground in a helpless heap was becoming a regular occurrence for him that day.

The Dark Man stood above him once again and crowed at the top of his voice. 'Here is your Prince,' he shouted, 'nothing more than a frightened child, when confronted by my might. Come and watch your saviour die. Come and watch your war end in defeat.' He raised the sword above his head once more and brought it down with all his might.

Lewis could do nothing but wait for the sword to strike. His head still swam and his limbs refused to obey his commands. He watched in horror as the sword fell towards him, light dancing across the blood covered blade. He desperately tried to raise a limb to protect himself, but it felt like a dead weight. As the sword came racing down, a flash of brown raced across his vision, taking it and The Dark Man away from him. Lewis blinked in surprise, and stared as his saviour, a brown lycan, attacked The Dark Man ferociously. Its attack had taken the monster by surprise. He was so focussed on killing Lewis that he never bothered to look up until it was too late. The lycan had managed to get inside his sword arm and was biting and clawing at the demon's body and face, ripping large gashes in his chest and leaving bite marks on his face. All The Dark Man could do was hammer at it with the sword hilt. Lewis shook his head and staggered to his feet. A wave of nausea flooded him, and he gagged and crouched down on all four paws. He looked up to see that The Dark Man had dropped his sword and had grabbed handfuls of fur with his now free hands. He was desperately trying to prise the lycan off him while it snapped and snarled, its claws raking across the demon's head and shoulders. The monster roared in pain and anger before finally managing to haul the lycan off and throwing it to the ground. The Dark Man jumped to his feet with preternatural speed, grabbing the sword as he did. The lycan wasted no time in rising off the floor and coming at the demon once again. The creature was ready this time and stepped forward, plunging the sword into the lycan's stomach as it dived towards its prey. The lycan slumped to the ground with a groan.

Lewis roared in fury and dived at the demon's back, punching him squarely between the shoulder blades, and sending him crashing to the ground. He jumped onto him before he could gain his feet and began to claw and bite at his exposed back and neck. The creature roared in anger and pain, somehow managing to swivel around on to his back and grabbing Lewis by the head. He pushed and twisted, his vice like grip managing to lift Lewis up and off him.

'Now it's your turn to feel pain,' he hissed as he began to push upwards. Somehow he lifted himself and Lewis up and off the ground, first by sitting up and then by getting his legs underneath him and pushing upwards until he was in a standing position with Lewis on his hind legs below him. The pressure on Lewis's head began to increase as the demon squeezed, a look of triumph spread across his bloody face. Lewis twisted and writhed below him, trying to snap at the hands either side of his head. His front paws were useless. He tried to push up from his hind legs, but The Dark Man was bearing down on him with all his weight. The pressure in his head increased and stars began to dance across his vision once again.

'What a pathetic creature you are. It's so easy to get the better of you. I shall enjoy your power. It will add to that of those who have gone before you. I'm sure Blaine never told you about them did he? They sustained us on this earth. They allowed us to plague mankind. Think about that. You and your kind are responsible for all the hurt we have done.'

The pressure and pain in Lewis's head increased and he could feel himself start to lose consciousness. He thought about changing back into his human form, but this would only make it easier for The Dark Man to crush his skull. This wasn't how this was supposed to happen. Lewis was the Prince of the Blood and so much stronger than any demon, so how had the monster got the better of him so quickly? The sword, a voice said inside his head. The sword gives them great power. Lewis realised his mistake too late. He should never have listened to Bob. It was too dangerous to face a demon holding a sword and The Dark Man had held two. He thought about Charlie and the danger she was now in by facing The Gatherer in his own lair, also holding two swords. There was nothing he could do to help her; he couldn't even help himself. He tried to focus on the monster in front of him and thought about the shrivelled heart inside its chest once again.

'That won't work this time. You're in your lycan form and your power is channelled into your strength. Blaine should have told you this.' The Dark Man said, laughing.

Lewis pawed pathetically at the creature's arms as consciousness slipped away. He was falling down a long tunnel into welcoming blackness. At least there would be no pain or hurt there.

With one final effort he managed to claw across The Dark Man's wrist. The creature grunted in pain then suddenly the pressure was released and Lewis fell backwards onto the floor, changing back into a human as he did. He swam in and out of consciousness for a few seconds, the shapes of fighting creatures swarming across his vision. They started to settle after what seemed an age and Lewis became aware of a dull ache throbbing on either side of his head. He looked up and tried to focus on the scene in front of him, his mind urging him to get up and protect himself. He was able to focus on the brown form of another lycan standing a few feet away from him, growling menacingly at an opponent behind Lewis. Ignoring the pain in his temples Lewis turned his head to see that The Dark Man stood a few paces away from him, looking intently at the lycan. He was bleeding from multiple cuts on his chest and face, but his eyes burned and his lips were pulled back in a sneer.

'You will not deny me my prey,' he hissed.

Lewis turned back to the snarling lycan but didn't recognise its markings.

'You dare to betray me this way?' the lycan barked in

response and jumped over Lewis to attack the demon.

Lewis scrambled to his feet and noticed the sword sticking out of The Dark Man's latest prey. He staggered towards it, grasping the hilt and drawing it out of the body. The weapon making a wct sucking sound as it came out. This was finally his chance. He had the sword and had transformed into a human. It was now or never. The Dark Man and the unknown lycan were engrossed in their battle to the death. Lewis stepped to the side, hefting the sword in his hand, feeling its weight and its power. A gentle hum went up his arm and into his shoulder. It dulled the pain in his temples and drew strength back into his limbs, while he watched and waited for an opening. He didn't want to stab his saviour by mistake. His chance came as the lycan fell to the floor. The Dark Man stepped forward and stamped down with his foot, exposing his chest. Lewis darted forward and plunged the sword into the creature's breast, hoping the tip would find its heart.

The Dark Man gave off a piecing howl that echoed across the underground station, ringing off the walls and bouncing off the floor. Every creature stopped what they were doing and turned towards the wounded demon. The hush that quickly descended was so complete that the only sound that remained was the painful sobs of The Dark Man. He grasped the hilt of the sword and tried to pull it out, but Lewis's aim had been true and the weapon refused to budge.

'No, no,' he gasped.

His death was quick. One moment he was kneeling on the floor, trying to remove the sword, the next his body trembled forward, hitting the cold floor with a loud thud.

All was quiet for a few seconds, then the remaining werewolves, realising their master was dead, started to run towards the exits.

The Dark Man's body began to tremble and shake, then fizz and pop. His form became a shimmering outline, then his body turned into dust that floated away, up into the dark roof of the station. The sword clanging to the floor once his body had disappeared.

Russell Brown

The cheering started at the far corner of the station and rolled forward like a wave of sound, catching up everyone in a scream of euphoria. Lewis stood in disbelief at first, not comprehending that he'd killed the demon. He looked up to see that his latest saviour, Beth, had changed back into human form and was smiling and laughing at him. The realisation of what had just happened hit him and he began to jump and dance like everyone else, the joy of the moment consuming him.

THE DEMON GATEKEEPER

Their swords clashed over and over again, sending blue sparks racing into the air each time they connected. Charlie could feel her arms burn with the effort of keeping The Gatherer at bay, there was a dull ache blooming between her shoulder blades, and her top was slick with sweat. His attacks had been ferocious, keeping her on the back foot and pushing her across the garbage strewn cavern. Her fellow lycans had stayed back, at her insistence. She needed to beat the monster herself. She desperately wanted to change and attack him but there was no way she could kill him in her lycan form. Bob had been clear on that point. You had to be a human to kill a demon. She had no idea why this would be the case, but she wasn't about to test the theory now. The demon came at her yet again, attacking with a series of hacks and thrusts that pushed her back against the wall. She rolled to her side an instant before his sword tip scraped the rock where she's been standing, and she managed to flick her sword upwards and nick his outstretched arm.

'You over-reached demon,' she gasped.

'You were lucky,' he replied.

Charlie back-tracked into the middle of the cave and let her arms fall at her side. 'Why only the one sword? I thought you had Blaine's too.'

'I only need one sword to beat you, my child. Talking to me so you can catch your breath only delays the inevitable. I do not want to take your life, but I will if you insist on trying to take my sword.'

'You're about the only monster who doesn't want to take my life.'

'Then why try to take mine?'

'Because you're a demon, hell spawn, and you don't belong on this earth.'

The Gatherer shook his head and came at her once again. Charlie was just about able to keep him at bay, but she was no master with a sword and knew she'd been lucky to survive so far, figuring her lycan strength and royal blood were helping her. His latest attack sent her to her knees. Without thinking she rolled over onto her side and tumbled across the floor, missing the tip of his sword by inches as he brought it down, again and again while she desperately tried to get away. Fi growled from the side line, and looked as if she was about to intervene.

'Stay out of the way, lycan, or you will feel my sword's bite.'

Charlie managed to get to her feet and spin to face the demon just as he launched another attack, this one as vicious as the last. The Gatherer hacked at Charlie's sword and tried to get inside her defences. She could feel her arms getting weaker with every blow, and the demon could too. A smile appeared through his greasy hair, and he suddenly stopped and stepped back.

'Have you had enough?'

Charlie put her hands on her knees and took in a lungful of air. 'Have you?'

'You cannot beat me, the sword gives me power greater than that of a royal princess, even one as stubborn as you. Why do you think we guard them so fiercely?'

'Your lot haven't been doing a good job of that lately,

we've managed to get loads of swords.'

'I didn't say my brothers were very good at it, especially when they're trapped in hell.'

'This only ends one way.'

'Yes, with your blood staining my cavern floor.'

Charlie was the first to attack this time, hoping to catch The Gatherer off guard. It didn't work. He easily parried her attack and made one of his own, pushing her back across the cavern and into the wall once again. Their swords met and The Gatherer pushed against them, leaning in and getting his face close to Charlie's. She tried not to gag at the odious stench that emanated from him, but she couldn't stop herself.

'Remember, it is the smell of truth, and the truth this time is that your life is about to come to an end. I will take your power reluctantly but be glad that it is me and not one of my brothers. I will use it to keep the portal closed and keep them out of this world.'

Charlie tried to push back, but the monster had his full weight bearing down on her now. Her sword started to bite into her chest and her senses began spinning as the air escaped from her lungs. She could hear her lycan comrades barking and snarling on the other side of the cavern but knew they would not interfere; she'd told them not to, no matter what happened. The Gatherer's dank hair touched her face and she shivered. It was a gruesome way to die, crushed to death by a smelly demon. She could feel the darkness start to creep over her. Her legs and fingers had gone numb, and the pain she felt in her chest and back started to recede. All she wanted was for the fight to end, and to lay down on the ground, even for a few minutes so she could get her breath back.

'Charlie, you need to open your eyes. You have to fight; he can't beat you if you believe in yourself. Open your eyes and fight, my love.' Her gran's voice was so close it felt like she could reach out and touch her.

'Come on, Charlie, he's nothing but a demon, open your eyes and I'll help you.'

Charlie opened her eyes to a vision full of dank hair, she

grimaced and started to push back. No smelly, unwashed demon was going to beat her.

'That's it, push, he won't be expecting you to fight back, and he won't be expecting me.'

A warm glow started to emanate from the hilt of Charlie's sword, it grew brighter and brighter until it formed a white light surrounding her. The Gatherer gasped and eased backwards, trying to get away from the glow. A sudden rush of air emanated from in front of Charlie and passed through the demon as he stepped backwards. He gagged and stumbled. This was the opening Charlie had waited for, she jumped forward and drove the sword point into the monster's chest. The blade pierced his heart and came out underneath his shoulder blades.

Charlie could just about see through his lank hair and make out the look of shock written across his face. He put a hand gently onto the blade sticking out of his chest, as if to see if it was real, then he grasped it in both hands and began to pull. The blade didn't budge and after a few seconds he let his hands fall to his sides.

'Why?' he asked in a whisper, shaking his head from side to side. 'All I wanted to do was protect you.'

'All you wanted to do was feed off the magic we create.'

The demon fell to his knees and started to shake. The skin on his arms and face began to bubble and steam lifted of his body. He groaned, before a hissing sound emerged from his lips, that quickly turned into a scream. His body went rigid, then fell onto the ground with a thump. The hissing stopped, his skin stopped trembling while the remaining steam rose up into the roof of the cavern and disappeared.

'Now what?' Fi asked. She'd changed back into her human form and stood warily near the entrance to the cavern.

'No!' the dirty man screamed as he rushed into the cavern and knelt down next to his dead master. 'What have you done? You stupid human, what have you done?'

'Rid the world of one more demon.'

'But you haven't, you idiot, you've made it a thousand times worse.'

'What are you talking about?'

'He was the Demon Gatekeeper. He was keeping the demons in hell. Why do you think there is so much rubbish in this cave?'

'Because he's a tramp as well as a demon.'

'No, you stupid child, it's all magic. He was using it to plug up the entrance to Hell. The one he's been sitting on all these years. If you value your lives, you need to get out of here now. Nothing will stop them coming through now. You've killed The Gatekeeper, you've unlocked the door.'

Charlie had no idea what the filthy little man was talking about, but anguish and fear were written across his face. She rushed forward and pulled the sword out of the demon's body and scooped up the other one that lay next to him. A wail came from the cavern entrance as the two headed dog scrambled over to the body and lay down next to it.

'I'm so sorry, master, they don't know what they've unleashed.'

The body started to hiss once again, then shake. The dog jumped away with a bark and the demon's servant stepped back. It continued to tremble, then fizz and pop until it became a shimmering outline that turned to into a cloud of dust that floated upwards into the dark roof of the cavern.

'So begins the dark night,' the servant mumbled.

'That's one down,' Charlie said.

'Many more are coming.'

The rumble began deep under the earth, a vibration that shook through the soles of Charlie's shoes. Stones and dirt began to fall from the walls and large rocks started to fall from high up in the roof.

'Watch out!' Fi yelled as the rain of rocks increased.

The litter scattered across the floor of the cavern started to shiver and quake, then swirl and jump as the grumbling under the earth increased and the floor shook. Charlie and her crew retreated to the relative safety of the entrance, but the dirty man and the dog refused to budge from where their master had disappeared.

A grating sound came from beneath the floor in the centre of the cavern, quickly followed by a shrill squeaking that made Charlie's ears hurt. Strange clicks like the sound of a rusty old lock being turned were next, then a sigh like the sound of a tomb being opened. The trembling stopped, as did the rain of rocks and earth. All the rubbish in the centre of the cave suddenly cascaded down a hole that had appeared in the centre of the floor, then all was silent as a grave.

Charlie could hear her heart beating as it fluttered wildly inside her chest. She wasn't sure what had just happened and prayed it had nothing to do with The Gatherer's demise. Killing him had been the right thing to do, he was hell spawn, an evil monster who wanted nothing more than to prey on the innocent beings living in her world. She couldn't allow that. She needed to rid the earth of all the demons and their devotees, never mind that God wanted a truce; that was just stupidity. This had been a good start, and yet a small part of her repeated the words that The Gatherer's filthy follower had said – you've killed The Gatekeeper, you've unlocked the door. So begins the dark night.

The two headed dog started to whine and paw at the ground. It growled and snarled, its hackles raised, and its many teeth bared. Then suddenly it turned around and ran out of the cave, barking and snarling.

'What the hell?' Fi said.

'Hell is right, lycan, you need to leave now if you value your life,' the filthy man said as he rose and made his way to the entrance.

'What do you think, Charlie?'

'He's bluffing,' Charlie said with a confidence she didn't feel.

'I don't know what the great big hole is, but it can't be good.'

'Must be something to do with that demon dying. He was probably keeping this dump together. I bet it will all fall apart now that his magic has gone.'

Charlie could hear a scratching sound coming from within the hole. It was soft at first but got louder and more insistent within a few heartbeats. It was followed by the sound of laughter. Not the hearty, full blooded laughter of friends at a party, but the nervous, eager laugh of someone worried about getting caught.

The drums started soon after, a steady booming sound like the toll of a bell mourning the dead.

'The drums are come from the deep, run, lycans, run for your lives,' the filthy man said from just outside the cave.

'Get ready,' Fi said, changing into her lycan form.

Charlie took in a deep breath and prepared herself for whatever was coming out of the hole.

Russell Brown

THE END AND THE BEGINNING

Lewis sat on the floor and shook his head. He'd done it, somehow, he'd done it. The Dark Man was dead. Not sent back to hell like before, but actually dead. Lycans all around him were dancing and patting each other on the back, while magical creatures of all shapes and sizes looked on confused, not sure if they should keep up their attacks or join in with the celebrations. He stared down at the sword cradled in his lap and smiled. It was the most beautiful thing he'd ever seen. An artefact of pure evil he knew he should destroy, but he couldn't get over how beautiful it was. There was at least another one somewhere on the platform. He knew he should look for it before it fell into the wrong hands, but he wanted to sit and admire the one in his lap for a bit longer. He could feel his weariness drain away the longer he kept in contact with the warm steel. The pain in his head and shoulders had already receded to a dull ache, and he was sure his cuts and bruises were healing rapidly. He wondered how Charlie was getting on with The Gatherer, and considered getting up to go and help her, but his eye caught a flash of light bouncing off the blade in his lap and he smiled and settled back to admire it a little more.

'That's not good for you,' a voice said from behind him.

'What do you mean?' Lewis asked without taking his eyes off the blade.

'That thing is cursed. It's a demon blade, pure evil, it will suck you in and never let you go.'

'It's making me feel better.'

'Of course, that's how it works. Put it down, Lewis.'

A hand reached over Lewis's shoulder and gently prised the blade from his grasp. Lewis wanted to protest, to stop the hand taking it, but he didn't know why and that terrified him. He let his grip go limp and watched with regret as the blade disappeared over his shoulder. He turned around to see Bob smiling at him. 'Well done.'

'We need to find the others.'

'We need to help the wounded first and someone needs to go and help Charlie.'

'Yep, and thank the crew, they were amazing,' Lewis said with a start, remembering the lycans that had saved him. He jumped up and saw one of them, Beth, walking towards him.

'Are you OK?' he asked as he reached her.

'I'm fine,' Beth said as she turned around. 'How are you?'

'I'll survive, thanks to you.'

'It was the least I could do. I'm sorry about earlier, I don't know what came over me, it was like someone was telling me I needed to kill you.'

'That was The Dark Man.'

'No, it was a female all covered in white.'

'Lightfoot,' Bob said shaking his head.

'Why?' Lewis asked.

'I don't know, but if an angel is working against us, we're in trouble. I know God wanted us to stop fighting, but I didn't think she's stoop to this level to stop us.'

'It might not have been at her command.'

'A rogue angel; we're in even more trouble than I

thought.'

'I think you better see if the other lycan is OK,' Beth said. 'She's in worse shape than me.'

Lewis suddenly remembered the first lycan who had saved him, the one he'd pulled the sword out of, and turned to find her. He spotted her lying on the floor, curled up with her back to him. He'd assumed she was dead when he'd pulled the sword out and felt a pang of guilt that his only thought at the time was to get the sword.

'Well, I was in a battle,' he murmured. 'Are you OK?' he asked as he knelt down to help her. The woman moaned and rolled over onto her back. All the feeling suddenly drained from Lewis's body as he stared down as his mother.

'No!' he hissed.

'Lewis,' his mother said weakly, before a raking cough rattled through her body.

'Mum,' was all he could say as he reached out and took her in his arms.

'Are you OK?' she asked in between coughs.

'Don't speak, you need to keep your strength, I'm going to get you to a hospital, mum, you're going to be OK. Someone help me, please!' he shouted.

'Oh, God, Scarlett,' Bob groaned as he reached Lewis's side.

'She's going to be OK! You're going to be OK, aren't you, mum?' Lewis said, the tears starting to fall from his face.

'Did you get him?'

'Yep, we got him, he's dead.'

'Good. I'm glad I could help you, my love. At least I could do that.'

'Please mum, don't talk, you need to lay still until we can get you some help.'

'It's OK love, it's what we do.'

'What is?'

'Die for our children.'

'You're not dying, I won't let you. You can't leave me.'

'I don't want to, but I think God is calling me now. I'll always watch over you.'

'I won't let you go. Someone, please, get help!' he shouted again before looking down into her glassy eyes and realising she'd gone.

'No, please, no,' he said, shaking his head. 'She didn't say goodbye, Bob, she needed to say goodbye.'

'I know, mate,' Bob said, putting an arm around him. 'Put her down Lewis, we'll take care of her now.'

Lewis let go of her, then covered his face in his hands. All he knew, in that moment, was pain and anguish. His mum was dead, and he'd not been able to save her. He was truly alone for the first time in his life. He was vaguely aware of Bob talking to him, and of other creatures surrounding him but he didn't care. His mum was gone, this whole thought consumed him as his body shook with grief.

It was the insistent pulling that finally brought him back to the present. Bob had grabbed him by the arms and was dragging him upwards.

'Get ready, form a line,' he was shouting to the lycans around him. 'Get ready, they're coming.'

Who was coming? Lewis wondered through his tears. What could possibly have gone wrong now?

'Change!' Bob screamed.

Lewis looked up to see a pack of demons racing towards him. They were snarling and screaming and he was sure at least one of them was laughing.

OUBLIETTE

E very part of Charlie ached. Her arms ached, her legs ached, her head ached, even her ears ached. She'd become use to pain, especially since discovering she was a lycan, but this was different. It felt like her whole body was broken from her head down to her toes. She knew she should try to move, to see if her suspicions were correct, but she couldn't even contemplate moving her eye lashes, never mind her legs or arms. The ground beneath her was cold and hard and a blackness enveloped her. She thought she'd managed to open her eyes but the dark was so total she couldn't be sure. After a few minutes she became aware of a weight pressing down on her legs. She tried to move one, but it wouldn't budge. Whether this was because of her weakened state, or because she was trapped, she didn't know. She tried desperately to remember what happened and how she'd got into this state, but her mind refused to concentrate at first, the cold and the pain consuming her. She closed her eyes and focussed her thoughts beyond the present, she had to remember what had happened. After a few seconds, she recalled the chaos in the cavern when the demons rushed out of the pit. Her comrades had fought valiantly, but no one had faced that many demons all at once and they'd quickly been overwhelmed. She had no idea what had happened to Fi, or the rest of them, but she remembered seeing plenty of blood. She'd lost the swords almost straight away, it was hard to hold anything when you were in lycan form, and had tried to fight, but facing off against two very angry demons quickly went bad. She'd been exhausted from the fight with The Gatherer, and was overwhelmed within minutes, falling to the ground with a demon on top of her. She'd looked up into the fierce red eyes and saw death waiting for her there. She remembered a strange calm had come over her at that point. If this was death, she was going to be reunited with her Gran, and that was no bad thing. It had been the giant that had saved her. It had hauled the demon off the top of her like it was no heavier than a feather and thrown it across the cavern. She remembered the giant had picked her up and put her on his shoulder, just like the last time, and they had somehow managed fight their way out of the cavern.

The chaos on the platform had been as bad as that in the cave. The werewolves, emboldened by the return of so many demons, were fighting with a ferocity she'd never seen before. The giant had ploughed a way through, fighting as he went. She'd tried to help but wasn't able to change back into a lycan while she was on his shoulders, and without the sword, was only able to swat away the odd attacking werewolf that got through the giant's defences.

She remembered they'd jumped off the end of the platform onto the old railway line, a pack of werewolves at their back. The giant had fought his way down the line, punching and kicking as he backed away. The dark had enveloped them as they went down the tunnel, the sounds of fighting bouncing off the walls. Charlie didn't know how long they'd fought for, but it had been terrifying, and she assumed, bloody. She remembered red eyes everywhere and the giant snarling and cursing. She could hear the sound of bodies as they were thrown against the tunnel walls and could feel the pain across her shoulders and back where the attacking werewolves had bitten her. The end came quickly. One minute they were fighting, the next they were falling, then all was blackness and she awoke in the dark.

After a few more minutes to steady her breathing, Charlie was able to slowly move her left hand, then her arm, each tiny movement sending pain shooting up into her shoulder and across her back. The movement left her feeling sick and she was desperate for a drink of water. She lay still until the nausea subsided then started moving her arm once again. She could feel the gritty earth beneath her palm, and the bumps and hollows of the ground she lay on. After a few more seconds her hand reached her face, and she gently probed the soft tissue of her cheeks and across her brow, wincing each time she found a cut or pressed down on a bruise. She was a mess and half glad she lay in total darkness. No doubt she would look a fright in the light.

She took in a deep breath and tried to move her legs once again but the weight across them was too much and all she managed to do was send fresh pain shooting across her body. Charlie felt frustrated by her current plight and frightened. If she didn't get herself out from underneath whatever it was that held her, she was going to die. There was no way they would ever find her in the dark tunnels, even if they knew where to start looking. No one had seen her and the giant disappear and it would be some time before they realised she was gone, if they had managed to escape the marauding demons first. She regretted what had happened in the cavern. Not that The Gatherer was dead, he was a monster and deserved his fate; she regretted what his death had led to. If they'd known what he was keeping at bay they would have tried to take the swords off him a different way, if there was one. Now the war had escalated, and Charlie wasn't sure if they could beat all the demons who had come through the portal. She wondered what had happened to Lewis, Bob and the rest of the crew, praying that they got out of the station safely.

'My, but you do look a mess.'

The sound startled her and she looked around for the source but all she could see was darkness.

'How did you get yourself down there?'

She realised the sound was coming from above, which meant that she was in some sort of hole.

'Do you know what they call these things, I bet you don't? Oubliette; it means a place of forgetting. It looks like you have been forgotten Charlie, what a shame.'

Horror bloomed in Charlie's chest as she recognised the voice to be that of Lewis's dad. 'What do you want?' she managed to croak, the effort sending fresh waves of pain across her body.'

'What do I want?' he asked himself. 'Let me see; world peace, an end to hunger, a stop to child slave labour ... oh, and your power. Not much really.'

Charlie's heart sank. She was down a hole, unable to move, too weak to change and at the mercy of a demon. Things weren't looking good.

'Don't worry, I'm not going to kill you, that would be counter-productive. I need you alive and making all that lovely blood power. We're going to have so much fun, you and I.'

She heard him shuffle about and his legs bang off the side of the hole as he sat down at the lip. 'That's better, we can have a proper chat now, oh, wait, let's shed some light on the subject, too.' A bright light burst across Charlie's vision, she winced and screwed her eyes shut.

'Don't worry, you'll get used to it. My, but you are in a predicament. You're trapped beneath a dead giant, that is a shame.'

Charlie groaned; her saviour had become her jailer.

'We'll need to do something about that, can't have you trapped, you'll never get better.'

'Why do you want me better?'

'Blood power, like I said. You'll make it and I'll drink it. It's going to be a special relationship.'

'You'll get nothing from me.'

'My dear Charlie, you don't get to choose. You're my prisoner now, I make the rules, besides, I could just leave you. There are rats down here bigger than dogs, did you know that? I think they'd find you a very tasty meal.'

Charlie shuddered at the thought but said nothing.

'Yes, I get to choose, and right now I choose to have a little chat. Don't you ever wonder about your blood power? Why you have it like you do but others don't? It's because you're born of a demon. I'm sure you already realised that when you found out Lewis was my son. Don't worry, I'm not your daddy, but I know who is.'

'Get lost.'

The demon chuckled, 'I think you're the one that's lost, but never fear, I'm here to help you. Yes, you are born of a demon, the last Princess of the Blood. I always thought God had a sick sense of humour. Making something so pure, out of something so dark. No doubt we could debate that one for ages, but there's so much more to tell.' He jumped down into the oubliette, landing on the ground next to Charlie with a thud.

'Let's see if we can't make you a bit more comfortable.'

Charlie felt the weight lift off her legs and groaned with the relief. It didn't last long, the pain quickly followed.

'Your legs look fine, just a bit of bruising; you're lucky, unlike the giant.'

Charlie listened as the demon lifted the giant's body, seemingly with ease, and threw it out of the hole. It landed some distance away with a soft thump.

'How can I do that?' the demon asked, pre-empting Charlie's question. 'It's your power my dear, it gives us so much more. Even in your weakened state, you are magnificent. Just wait until you've recovered. Now, let me help you up.' He grabbed her gently under the arms and lifted her into a sitting position. Waves of nausea and pain flooded her body. She flopped back against the wall and waited for them both to subside.

'Now,' he said, settling in on the opposite side of the oubliette, 'let's talk.'

'What about?'

'You, lycans, werewolves, all that stuff.' You do realise we have entered the end game?'

Charlie shook her head in response.

'You've killed The Gatherer, and that means all my brothers are free to roam this earth and cause all kinds of terrors. I myself am thrilled at the prospect. We have coveted this plane for millennia and now we are free to wander; it's a great thing you have given us, Charlie, a truly great thing.'

Charlie tightened her lips and refused to respond. He was a demon and lying was as natural to him as breathing.

'We will pillage and rape and feed, it will be wonderful, and we have a readymade army of werewolves to help us. It couldn't be better. Do you know what they really are? I bet you've wondered. The truth is, there is no difference between lycans and werewolves. They chose to follow my brothers, while you chose to follow the light. It's as simple as that. They're nothing special really. We give them red eyes, so we know the difference. I bet you thought they were demon spawn, hellish creatures, but no, it is their choice to follow us. How does it make you feel, to know your fellow creatures prefer to service us.'

'I don't care.'

'I think you do, I think it's eating you up inside. Everyone must choose a path in life, theirs is just different from yours.'

'No one chooses to follow a demon.'

'But that's where you're wrong, you did. Good, evil, there's no difference in the end. It's all about power and who has it. You could choose to follow me anytime?'

'I'll never follow you.'

'That's a shame; not to worry, you'll change your mind eventually.'

'I don't think so, demon.'

'We can't have you calling me that, it's so impersonal. Shall I tell you my real name? Why not, we're going to get to know each other well. I have many names, as do my brothers, but you will know me best as Lucifer, the Prince of Darkness, the morning star, the fallen angel himself.'

'Whatever.'

Lucifer chuckled, 'I love your spirit, Charlie, don't ever

lose it. It makes your power so much sweeter. She cast me down long before man could speak. I was part of her heavenly host, a mighty cherubim, and she cast me down for doubting her. All I did was ask questions, something you do all the time. She's a cruel God, Charlie, cruel to her servants. I would never cast you out.'

'You're a liar. I know your story. You were full of pride and lusted after power. Your actions started a war in heaven.'

'Just the twisted stories of Dante and Chaucer, I'm afraid, all lies.'

'I don't think so,' Charlie replied, shuffling her aching legs and trying to get into a more comfortable position.

'I can take away your pain you know. A flick of my wrist and you'll be all better. I can show you how to channel your power too. I can make you more powerful than you ever thought possible. Just follow me and I'll show you all.'

'Still lusting after power, I see. Like I said, I'll never follow you, demon. I'd die first.'

'Oh, well, I tried,' Lucifer said, shaking his head. 'If you want to do this the hard way that's your choice. I will take your power either way, but it is sweeter if freely given, just remember that.'

'You'll get nothing from me.'

'We'll see, Charlie, we'll see.'

PARLEY

There had been a place of worship on the same ground since the Middle Ages, a sacred place where pilgrims could come and worship God. Whether she was listening was another matter, but they had come in their droves, and knelt and prayed. Pleading for a cure, or for riches, or for a newer, better-looking wife or husband. All types had come and gone over the ages. The original church had been built at the time of the reformation, but that had been burnt to the ground and a newer church had now taken its place. That too had been abandoned for over thirty years, and was gently falling back into the earth.

Jillian remembered when the place had been full of worshipers. She remembered the famous minister John Knox screaming from the pulpit, looking down on all his wide-eyed parishioners and warning them of the dangers of sin. She remembered the weddings and the funerals, the cheering and the crying. She loved to hide out in churches back then, it was the one place God never thought to look for her. She remembered the last time she'd been on this site. It had been in the old church, long before this one had been built. The preacher had asked her to marry him, and she'd laughed, a dangerous thing for a woman to do back then. He'd called her a hag and told her she'd never get a good man. He'd been right on that score, she preferred a good woman anyway. Jillian sighed and sat down on a broken pew. She didn't know why she'd agreed to Blaine's parley, he'd only lie or try to steal something from her, but she'd been intrigued when she found out that lycans were to be present too. She could finally confront the ancestor of her lover's killer.

'There's still something about the place, isn't there?' a voice said from behind her.

'It's sacred, even though humans have abandoned it.'

'What fools they are.'

'Why have you called me here?'

'To parley of course.'

'We have nothing to talk about.'

'I don't know about that; I would have thought that you and Lewis would have plenty to talk about?'

'That's between me and him, demon.'

Blaine smiled as he walked down the aisle, hopping over rubbish and side stepping around a bit of fallen masonry.

'We'll see,' he said, before taking a seat on the opposite side of the aisle.

'I bet our friend Derek would have loved this place.'

'I don't know who that is,'

'Just some lost soul my brother killed.'

'Your kind are very good at killing.'

'And this coming from a servant of God. We're amateurs compared to her.'

Jillian sighed then pursed her lips. 'You're wasting my time,' she said, standing up.

'Maybe, but I'm sure they won't,' he replied, pointing towards the door as Bob and Lewis entered. Jillian ground her teeth and clenched her fists.

'This is a sacred place and under parley remember,' Blaine warned her.

Tensions sparked as Lewis saw Blaine and Jillian. His face was set in a determined stare and his fists were balled just like the angel's.

'What do you want?' he said, stopping halfway down the aisle.

'Welcome to this sacred place, my Prince of the Blood,' Blaine said with a flourish. 'It's good to see you once again.'

'I can't say the same demon. Get on with it before I rip your head from your body.'

'I'm sure Bob will have already told you that this is a sacred place so no fighting, members of our little group are protected under the ancient rules of parley, so once again, no fighting.'

'He did, what do you want?'

'I'm sorry for your loss, Lewis, truly I am. I liked Scarlett, she was a friend.'

'Do not speak her name!' Lewis hissed, stepping forward with a face like thunder. Bob took him gently by the shoulder and pulled him backwards.

'Very well, but I'm sorry all the same. I have called you to this place so you can hear my words. You have killed my brother Baal and set my family free. This was a reckless action that puts every human on this planet in danger. You must know by now that Baal was the plug, the keeper of the keys, the barrier against the storm. He kept my brothers from this world and kept you all safe. Now he is gone.'

'There seemed to be plenty of you in our world while he was alive, he wasn't doing that good a job,' Bob said.

'There are many ways into this world. Not all of them can be plugged, but Baal stopped most; now they are open and you will reap the consequences.'

'No doubt you have a plan to stop all this?' Jillian said.

'I do, but it will take courage and no a small amount of magic.'

'You're after blood power,' Lewis said, 'this is all a ruse to get more blood power for yourself. Do you think we will fall for that again? Every lycan wants to kill you on sight.'

'This is not about blood power, it's about stopping my brothers.'

'How?'

'Baal is gone, but I am here. Help me find his sword,

and mine, and I will take over his place in the cavern. I will plug the entrance and send my brothers back to hell.'

'You're an opportunist, I'll give you that,' Bob said. 'You've probably looked for your own sword already and can't find it.'

'You know we worked well together for years, Bob; how many battles did I help you win? Did I let my brothers through the gate?'

'It was all a sham so you could keep the power for yourself, just like you're trying to do now.'

'Yes, it will give me power, I don't deny it, but it will give you peace as well. I make the offer under parley and ask you to go away and consider it.'

'And why am I here?' Jillian asked.

'As a witness from God. I know she wants an end to the wars, and all that has happened is that the fighting has gotten worse. I offer a way out, a way to peace. If the angels could help, if they could fight on our side, then we will have enough power to beat my brothers and send them back to the pit. Help me find the swords and we can confront them all in one last battle, angels, lycans and a demon all together. Surely this is what God wants?'

'Don't presume to know her mind,' Jillian warned him.

'It's the way of peace, why would she not agree?'

'It's a way for you to get what you want at everyone else's expense,' Lewis said. He'd been shaking with rage ever since he'd entered the church. It took all his strength not to dive at the demon and the treacherous angel. He felt hollow since his mum's death, and Charlie's disappearance, like a part of him had disappeared, leaving just an empty space behind. He wanted to scream and shout and cry, but he could do none of these things while a horde of demons walked the earth. So he'd tried desperately to put his worries to one side and concentrate on the here and now, but it was hard when the here and now contained the very creatures that had helped to kill his mother and Charlie's gran, and were probably involved in Charlie disappearance.

'This is a treacherous angel, she shouldn't be here, she

doesn't represent God any more than I do,' Lewis spat.

'I'm no more treacherous than you, human.'

'What are you talking about?'

'Your mother and I had a little chat before she died, I guess you didn't know that. I told her all about her ancestors, one in particular, who killed my partner. He accused her of being a witch and they hanged her, all the while hiding the fact that he was a filthy lycan. I swore then that I would have my revenge, I'm only sorry I wasn't able to finish her off before The Dark Man did.'

'Stop!' Blaine said, divining in front of Lewis before he changed into a lycan. 'This is sacred ground, you will not spill blood.'

'You might be safe now, but I'm coming for you.'

'I've waited for centuries to have my revenge, I can wait a little longer. It was me that told The Dark Man about your spies too, Bob, that Scarlett had returned, and where he could find her. Finish your parley, Blaine. I grow tired of this human.'

Bob and Lewis started forward, murder in their eyes.

'Stop!' Blain shouted. 'We are in parley, you will not fight.' He sighed when Bob pulled Lewis back. 'Can we not agree to put our differences aside and fight a common enemy?'

'You are the enemy, Blaine, you and your brothers, we see no difference between you. I'm going to kill you and then I'm going to deal with this angel. I'm sorry that you lost a loved one,' he said, turning towards Jillian, 'but from what you say that was centuries ago. I can't be held to account for the evils of my ancestors, but you can for the evil you do here and now. You betrayed Bob and me, tried to kill my mother, and no doubt will still try to kill me. I thought you were an agent of God, but I can see now that you are simply an agent for yourself.'

'You have no concept of the pain your family has caused me, lycan. I am eternal and my pain lives with me always. Your death and the death of all your family is a balm to that pain. I will look forward to taking your life. Look to defend yourself, for we will not parley the next time we meet.' With that Jillian turned and walked down the aisle, and out over the cracked alter.

'Well, that went well,' Bob said. 'Now it's your turn, Blaine, or Asmodius or whatever you call yourself. Parley is over.'

'I'm sorry we cannot come to an accord; please remember I tried.' He nodded to them both and left.

'The nerve of that guy. He comes straight out of hell and thinks he can negotiate with us while his brothers are about to cause havoc,' Bob said.

'It's in his nature, he's a demon,' Lewis replied.

'We know what he is this time, and he'll get no help from us. We better go, we still haven't found Charlie or some of the others.'

Lewis's heart sank at the thought of Charlie, lost or – worse – dead. 'Have we cleared all the bodies yet?'

'Yeah, most of them, she's not among them, thank God.'

'Did we lose many?'

'Far too many.'

'What's next?' Lewis asked, knowing the answer.

'We have to bury her, mate. We have to bury them all.'

'Won't the police grow suspicious with all these people disappearing.'

'No,' Bob replied with a scoff, 'most of us live on the edge of their world, leaving as little behind as we can. Your mum was the same.'

Lewis tried not to cry but he felt the tears come anyway. 'I don't think I'm ready to say goodbye just yet,' he said.

'I know, but your mum would have wanted you to move on. Come on, let's get back to the shop. We need to make sure Blaine isn't trying to take it back, and I'm gagging for a cup of tea.'

JAMIE AND THE TREE

J amie stood and stared. His brain told him his eyes were telling the truth, but he wasn't sure he believed them. The sight in front of him was the most amazing thing he'd ever seen. It must be a dream, nothing this wonderful could be true. A large cavern stretched out before him, its massive roof arching over his head, the top just visible in the far distance. The cavern floor was full of small houses, penned livestock, a meandering river and green hills peppered with daffodils. As amazing as all this was, especially when Jamie considered they were directly below the city centre, it was the tree that took his breath away. It sat on top of a large hill at the very centre of the cavern, easily a hundred feet tall, its branches reaching out across the empty space and giving shade to the buildings surrounding it. Its leaves were the colour of molten gold, russet red and emerald green, and a soft light seemed to radiate from its centre, bathing the whole cavern in a warm glow.

'Isn't it amazing?' Silas asked.

'It's the most fabulous thing I've ever seen,' Jamie replied, without taking his eyes off the tree.

'Would you like to get a closer look?'

Jamie nodded and they began to descend into the cavern.

'Who are all these people?' Jamie asked as they passed a house full of noisy creatures.

'We're satyrs, half human, half goat.'

'Why are you all here?'

'To look after the tree of course?'

'All of you just to look after one tree?'

'It's a very special tree, Jamie.'

They crossed a bridge spanning the river and Jamie looked down to see a woman rise up out of the water and do a back flip, before disappearing back into its depths. She had long golden hair and a fin where her legs should be.

'Was that a mermaid?'

'Yes,' Silas replied, 'many magical creatures call the cavern home, but satyrs have a special place here, we are the keepers of the tree.'

Jamie shook his head for the millionth time that day. He knew this should all be a dream, but it was real. He wondered what the surviving members of Abandoned Glasgow would think if they saw the cavern. 'Maybe we should have a special outing,' he thought to himself, chuckling at the idea of bringing his friends to such an amazing place.

They reached the bottom of the hill the tree sat on and began to make their way upwards. After a few minutes Jamie became aware of the sound of singing filling his ears. He looked around but could see no choir. The music grew louder as they climbed the hill, a rich, velvety sound so beautiful it made him want to cry with joy.

'What is that sound?' he managed to croak.

'The tree, it's reaching out to you.'

They eventually reached the massive bole and Jamie looked up into its mighty branches with awe. Nothing this massive could ever be alive in the real world. Without thinking he placed his hands onto the trunk and an enormous sense of wellbeing enveloped him. He felt loved and protected, cherished and appreciated, in a way his parents had never managed. He leaned in and placed his forehead on the trunk, letting out a sigh as he did.

'Welcome Jamie,' the tree whispered, 'you are safe here.'

'Thank you,' he managed to say before his emotions overtook him once again, and tears spilled from his cheeks.

'Do not cry, it will all be well. I have a message for you, Jamie, a message you must take to the others.'

'What message?'

'Tell them they are coming. It is time, and they are coming.'

'Who is coming?'

'Don't worry, they will know.'

'Who will?'

'The prince and princess. I also have a message for another,' the tree said, sending an image into Jamie's mind.

Jamie sighed and lifted his head off the tree. 'Do I need to go and tell them now?'

'Yes.'

'Can't I stay a little longer?'

'No, you must pass on the message, time is short and they need to be warned.'

Jamie nodded and stepped back from the tree. Reluctantly he peeled his eyes off the magnificent sight and walked back to Silas. The satyr nodded and led him back down the hill.

'I have to leave.'

'I assumed you would have to.'

'The tree's alive.'

'Of course it is.'

'And it talked to me,'

'Of course it did, what did you expect, it's a magic tree?'

'I suppose,' Jamie said, laughing.

Silas placed a hand on Jamie's shoulder and led him back to the exit, the light of the tree casting a warm glow as they made their way out.

End of Book Two

Other titles by BLKDOG Publishing for your consideration:

Arthur: Shadow of a God
By Richard Denham

King Arthur has fascinated the Western world for over a thousand years and yet we still know nothing more about him now than we did then. Layer upon layer of heroics and exploits has been piled upon him to the point where history, legend and myth have become hopelessly entangled.

In recent years, there has been a sort of scholarly consensus that 'the once and future king' was clearly some sort of Romano-British warlord, heroically stemming the tide of wave after wave of Saxon invaders after the end of Roman rule. But surprisingly, and no matter how much we enjoy this narrative, there is actually next-to-nothing solid to support this theory except the wishful thinking of understandably bitter contemporaries. The sources and scholarship used to support the 'real Arthur' are as much tentative guesswork and pushing 'evidence' to the extreme to fit in with this version as anything involving magic swords, wizards and dragons. Even Archaeology remains silent. Arthur is, and always has been, the square peg that refuses to fit neatly into the historians round hole.

A Storm of Magic
By Ashley Laino

Being brought back from the dead is an impressive trick, even for magician Darien Burron. Now he must try and use his sleight of hand to swindle modern-day witch, Mirah, to sign her power away, or end up a tormented demon in the afterlife.

Meanwhile, sixteen-year-old Mirah is starting to lose control of her powers. After an incident at her aunt's Witchery store, Mirah is sent to a secret coven to learn to control her abilities. While away, Mirah meets up with a soft-spoken clairvoyant, a brazen storm witch, and the creator of dark magic itself. The young woman must learn to trust in herself before she loses herself entirely to the darkness that hunts her.

Weirder War Two
By Richard Denham & Michael Jecks

Did a Warner Bros. cartoon prophesize the use of the atom bomb? Did the Allies really plan to use stink bombs on the enemy? Why did the Nazis make their own version of Titanic and why were polar bear photographs appearing throughout Europe?

At a time of such enormous crisis, scientists sought ever more inventive weapons, or devices to help halt the war. Civilians were involved as never before, with women taking up new trades, proving themselves as capable as their male predecessors whether in the factories or the fields.

The stories in this book are of courage, of ingenuity, of hilarity in some cases, or of great sadness, but they are all thought-provoking - and rather weird. So whether you are interested in the last Polish cavalry charge, the Blackout Ripper, Dada, or Ghandi's attempt to stop the bloodshed, welcome to the Weirder War Two!

Click Bait
By Gillian Philip

A funny joke's a funny joke. Eddie Doolan doesn't think twice about adapting it to fit a tragic local news story and posting it on social media.

It's less of a joke when his drunken post goes viral. It stops being funny altogether when Eddie ends up jobless, friendless and ostracized by the whole town of Langburn. This isn't how he wanted to achieve fame.

Under siege from the press, and facing charges not just for the joke but for a history of abusive behavior on the internet, Eddie grows increasingly paranoid and desperate. The only people still speaking to him are Crow, a neglected kid who relies on Eddie for food and company, and Sid, the local gamekeeper's granddaughter. It's Sid who offers Eddie a refuge and an understanding ear.

But she also offers him an illegal shotgun - and as Eddie's life spirals downwards, and his efforts at redemption are thwarted at every turn, the gun starts to look like the answer to all his problems.

Burning Bridges
By Chris Bedell

They've always said that three's a crowd...

24-year-old Sasha didn't anticipate her identical twin Riley killing herself upon their reconciliation after years of estrangement. But Sasha senses an opportunity and assumes Riley's identity so she can escape her old life.

Playing Riley isn't without complications, though. Riley's had a strained relationship with her wife and stepson so Sasha must do whatever she can to make her newfound family love and accept her. If Sasha's arrangement ends, then she'll have nothing protecting her from her past. However, when one of Sasha's former clients tracks her down, Sasha must choose between her new life and the only person who cared about her.

But things are about to become even more complicated, as a third sister, Katrina, enters the scene...

EST. 2019

BLKDOG

www.blkdogpublishing.com